Priests of Moloch

This book is a work of fiction. Any resemblance to actual events or persons, living or dead, is entirely coincidental.

"Priests of Moloch," by Samuel Schiller. ISBN 1-58939-928-5.

Published 2006 by Virtualbookworm.com Publishing Inc., P.O. Box 9949, College Station, TX 77842, US. ©2006, Samuel Schiller. All rights reserved. No part of this publication may be reproduced, stored in a retrieval system, or transmitted in any form or by any means, electronic, mechanical, recording or otherwise, without the prior written permission of Samuel Schiller.

Manufactured in the United States of America.

Priests of Moloch

Samuel Schiller

Also by Samuel Schiller

Warrior of the Son

Artwork by Laurie Gowland

To Robin Hardy.
For your giving nature, patience and
enthusiasm, I will always be indebted.

GLENMARA

UNCHARTED LANDS

RIVER AIDAS
LOCH AIDAS
HALD MOUNTAINS

FALTHEGEN

GOTH
LOCH CUINN
GWENFEREW

RIVER CUINN
DURHAM
GLENRE
JAYFELD

RIVER CAIRLATHE

 CARONE

EONACHT

RIVER OETH
FALLS OF WESTERFIELD
MOUNTAINS OF CARLATHE
CARONIAS PASS

ONDRIA

CHAPTER I
Reunion

It was dark there, deep beneath the mountains of Iarlaithe, too dark even for the keen and cunning eyes of goblins, so they had kindled torches and thrust them into cracks and niches in the cavern wall. There, beyond the reach of the sun, hundreds of goblins had gathered.

They were Grey Goblins with dull grey flesh and an attendant stench that coiled through the air to overpower the smell of mud and dark rock. Pale orange eyes darted furtively about the cavern. Goblin voices whispered.

"Best ta go home," they said.

"Poor doins if'n we stays," they complained.

"Ain't no reason ta go on," they insisted.

Atop a large, flat rock, a mottled, grey-brown goblin paced back and forth on short legs while gesturing wildly with his long, powerful arms.

"He ain't comin' back, I say. That human boy done killed 'im. Time ta go home."

Then another goblin, unlike any there, pushed his way through the crowd to the base of the rock. Tall and man-like, his skin shone a dull, copper-red in the torchlight, contrasting sharply with the coarse, dark hair that hung in a single braid across a broad, mailled shoulder. Thin lips curled back in an unpleasant snarl while bright yellow eyes glared at those about him. Whispers stilled, darting eyes averted, and the Grey Goblins shifted from side to side in a nervous mimic of their normal gait. "Runnin' away, Morg?" the Red Goblin snarled, "After all this way? She-goblin!"

Morg laid a long-fingered hand to the hilt of his sword. "If yer insults me again, Klabaga, I'll kill yer!" he warned.

Klabaga sneered, "Yer'll never do it! The whole lot of yer 'ave gone coward since the human boy killed the Glamorth!"

A collective shudder rippled through the crowd at the sound of that last word, and even Morg took a step back as though staggered by the vision it conjured.

"No ordinary human boy, that!"

"Not ordinary?" scoffed Klabaga. "I looked him right in the eye, didn't I? And didn't he run when the Glamorth came? That's ordinary enough, ain't it?"

"He ran right to that bridge and fought with but rocks. And anyhow, if there weren't nuthin' special 'bout him, why didn't yer kill him when yer was 'lookin' him right in the eye'?"

Klabaga shrugged. "The Glamorth wanted him. Anyhow, some of yer got too eager, and the human boy gave 'em what fer."

"That's what I'm sayin!" enthused Morg, "He must've killed twenty and wounded more'n that. I sez we go home ta our wives and children afore we end up dead."

Klabaga trembled with rage at the cowardice of his companions, but he knew Morg was right about one thing; there was nothing ordinary about Evan MacKeth. Beyond the flesh and blood and bone burned a fierce, unfamiliar light, and Klabaga suspected it was that light that had enabled the human boy to destroy the Glamorth. But the death of the demon didn't change the plans of the Red Goblin. "Yer afraid of a dead human boy? What's he got ta do with the rest of us?"

"I dunno," puzzled Morg. Even Klabaga wondered why the Glamorth had been so determined to kill Evan MacKeth, and why the boy had ventured into the dark underworld in the first place. "But it don't make no never mind. I'm Chieftain now and we is going' home!"

"So you're Chieftain? Then I gives the challenge!"

The other goblins had just begun to make room when Morg leapt upon Klabaga with a howl, driving his opponent to the cavern floor. The spectators scattered as the pair kicked and bit and gouged at one another in a violent tangle at their feet. Shouting and jostling, the Greys took up positions to watch the fight.

Klabaga drove his knee into Morg's belly, but hard muscle and maille deflected the blow. Despite their appearance, there was nothing soft about Grey Goblins. Morg pounded his long-fingered fists into the Red Goblin's face, clawed at his eyes and bit at his arms like a wild beast, but there was nothing soft about Klabaga either. He kicked his opponent in the throat and disengaged.

Scrambling to his feet, Klabaga parried Morg's blade, and the Greys hooted with delight as the cavern echoed with the sound of steel against steel. Morg feinted low, reversed his wrist and aimed a terrific blow at Klabaga's chest, but this too his opponent avoided before blocking another wild slash calculated to decapitate him. Someone shoved the Red Goblin from behind, propelling him into his enemy, and for a moment they grappled in a macabre dance.

The Grey pulled free, struck at Klabaga's face with his sword hilt, and followed with a quick succession of blows that increased in speed and intensity as his enemy steadily retreated. Morg's face twisted into a crooked grin as he sensed victory: Klabaga was barely holding his own. But then the Red Goblin stopped, his eyes glinted as though amused, and suddenly Morg's attack degenerated into a desperate defense.

The goblin commander staggered from the power and precision of the martial skill that Klabaga now turned against him, and in that despairing instant he realized his opponent had merely been toying with him. Now the game was over. Morg cast about for an escape, turned to seek refuge in the sea of swaying grey shapes surrounding him and fell in a gout of dark blood, never to rise again.

With a movement, as precise as it was brutal, Klabaga severed Morg's head from his body. Holding the grisly trophy aloft, he addressed the crowd. "Who's Chieftain now?" he challenged, "Answer me, ya slack jawed lot! Who's Chieftain?"

"Yer is!" asserted the closest goblin, trying to stay clear of Klabaga's crimson smeared sword.

"That's right!" the Red Goblin crowed, "and which of yer will challenge? Yer, Orglyx? Yer, Glak?"

Klabaga leapt up onto the rock. "Who wants ta go home now? Show me the goblin what wants ta go home!" No one responded.

"Did ya come all this way cuz of the Glamorth? I don't think so. Why'd ya come?" He searched the faces of the huddled crowd, but there was no sign of understanding in those dull eyes. The Greys cast anxious glances about the chamber as though searching for answers among the rocks. Why *had* they come? It seemed just a great bother now, especially with all these questions.

Klabaga knew what had brought them: fear. The demon had come recruiting warriors, and this lot hadn't dared refuse. But the Red Goblin had different motivations and a distinct purpose for this journey. The Greys, though they were ignorant, were necessary for what he had in mind.

"I knows why yer here," he offered, and the Grey Goblins looked up, eager to accept insight into their own behavior. "Vengeance brung ya; vengeance fer yer da's and granda's, yer cousins and uncles what was kilt by the da's and granda's, cousins and uncles of that dead human boy!

"Vengeance yer'll find in Ugrik's army when we burns the man-city of Gwenferew. That's why yer came this far, and that's why yer'll go farther. It's jest the beginning, the start of our time, when we takes war ta the world of human men."

The Greys began to stir, snarling, hissing, and shoving one another as their lust was stirred by the Red Goblin's words. He led them further.

"She-goblins will sing songs 'bout us and elders will offer us their daughters. They'll carve our names on the Clan Pillar. Follow me, and yer'll have human slaves fer yer pleasure, human skulls fer yer pillows, human blood ta spice yer gholjaka. Else run home and have nothin'! Red death ta human men!"

"Red death! Red death!" the Grey's replied.

"Ulu! Ulu! Ulu!" they chanted.

"Who follows me?" demanded the Red Goblin, and the cavern erupted with eager exclamations of support. Goblins danced madly about the chamber as though they had never wavered in their focus or desire.

Klabaga shouted orders as he sheathed his bloody sword. Then he led his soldiers north through the dark underworld toward a place called Clon Miarth to find cruel revenge and a reckoning with fate.

The king of Glenmara lay dreaming. Had he been aware of it, he would have thought it remarkable that he slept at all, for his heart had been so heavy and his spirit so troubled that the blissful release of sleep eluded him.

But now he dreamed many things in the cold chill of night--things that haunted his past and clouded his future, things that held him prisoner and tortured his soul. He dreamed of the bitter, dark days before his ascension to the throne when he had surrendered his half-brother Evan to the priests of Moloch for torture and death. He revisited the sad place where in a reckless instant he had murdered Evan's mother and placed a price on Evan's head. He called out in the depth of these remembrances as though in crying out against them now he might somehow alter his folly. But there was no erasing what he had done, or the effect it had visited on so many others. His dream moved on to other landscapes of nightmare and sorrow.

The healing grace of the One True God had eventually changed his vengeful spirit, but he had continued to search for Evan, to try, if it were possible, to make amends for all the evil he had done. Then, unexpectedly, miraculously, word had come of Evan MacKeth's capture.

Prepared for death, Osric had surrendered himself to Evan's justice, yet such was the power of the Holy Spirit that the reunion had instead brought salvation, and the fragile hope that the pair might somehow salvage their relationship. But with hardly any explanation at all, Evan had departed for the Mountains of Iarlaithe. Now, with weeks gone by and no word of his sibling, still the comforting oblivion of sleep eluded Osric.

But he slept now, and after a time his dreams brought him to a quiet place filled with peaceful whispers and inhabited by an extraordinary vision.

———————

When the king woke in the cold light of the winter dawn, he was reluctant to stir from the comfort of his bed. But as his mind began to focus, the familiar ache of guilt and doubt returned, leaving no possibility of more sleep.

Osric pulled back the embroidered woolen blankets, parted the elaborate bed curtains and looked out into the room. He found Ivrian in a cushioned chair, her golden hair reflecting the dancing radiance of the newly kindled fire. He went to her, stroked her cascading tresses.

She smiled and nuzzled his hand. "Did you sleep well, my love?"

Osric sighed, "Yes, but such dreams!"

He slid into the chair beside her, pressing against her warmth, and for a time they simply enjoyed the quiet presence of each other.

"I prayed for your brother last night," Ivrian finally said, "but it was for you, poor husband, that the prayer was meant. Finding Evan hasn't eased your anguish. I would that you forget him, since his remembrance serves you so ill."

Osric started to answer but Ivrian quickly placed a finger against his lips. "I know, my love," she said, "I know. So I prayed for Evan last night. I wish him no ill, but 'tis you I worry over." She kissed him. "Now tell me of your dreams."

Osric knit his brow, puzzling out the vague remembrance. "I know it had to do with Evan, but I could never quite understand it." He paused, searching his thoughts. "A bird. There was a bird, perched on the bedpost and it was talking to me. Can you imagine such a thing?"

Ivrian pushed away. "What sort of bird?"

"A funny bird. I think it was black and red. Why? Where are you going?"

Ivrian raced to a small table near the fireplace, returning excited, breathless. "I found this at the foot of the bed when I woke," she said, holding out a purple-black feather, tipped in bright crimson.

As Osric took the feather in his trembling hand, so the dream burst into his mind, and in that instant he knew. "My horse!" he roared, flinging open the chamber door. "My horse!" cried he to the startled guards, "and summon my surgeon! There is not a moment to be lost!"

———————

Braced in the doorway of his cabin, Rolfe watched the steady parade of horsemen file into the clearing, their steeds lathered and snorting, their maille jingling softly in the cool, heavy air of evening. Brightly painted shields hung from their saddles, and pennants streamed from the shafts of lances whose polished blades shone like mirrored silver in the last fading light of the dying day. After everything else that had occurred over the past week, Rolfe wasn't surprised at the arrival of this magnificent entourage.

From amongst this throng, a figure in dark armor approached the cabin. His garments were finer, his weapons richer than any there, and even Rolfe could tell he was a man of some importance. An immense warrior on a horse of like size and a grey bearded man who wore a simple skullcap of unbleached wool, accompanied him.

"Where is my brother?" the figure demanded.

Rolfe bowed. "I don't know your brother, lord, but there's a hurt boy in my cabin."

He had not yet straightened when the trio pushed past him into the cabin. The large warrior seized Rolfe by the collar as he passed, and pulled him inside.

"If you've done the lad any mischief I'll see to you myself," he whispered.

"I do him mischief?" countered Rolfe, trying to pull away from his captor. "I found him that way. I don't even know who he is!"

"He's Evan MacKeth, King Osric's brother."

"King Osric? King Osric did you say?"

"King Osric," insisted the warrior, tugging harder at Rolfe's collar, "right there in your cabin!" He pointed to one of the men on the far side of the room, and Rolfe would have fallen to his knees were it not for the warrior's unwelcome support.

The warm flush of fear rushed through Osric at the sight of his brother lying motionless on the bed of moldy straw. He was covered with bruises and cuts that contrasted sharply with his pale flesh, and for a startling moment the king despaired that Evan yet lived. But at last the young man took a struggling breath. Osric twisted at his sword belt while the man in the wool skullcap examined the stricken youth. "What say you, Torgal?" the king asked at length.

Torgal Umliath, physician to the Royal house of Murchadha, removed a bony hand from Evan's forehead and turned a grim face to his king. "It isn't good." He pulled aside the crude bandage on Evan's shoulder to reveal a mass of angry red flesh. "He is fiercely wounded. His leg is broken, and there is fever. He doesn't even know we're here."

"Can you save him?"

Torgal frowned. "He has other wounds that are barely healed. What mischief has befallen him I can only guess!"

"Can you save him?" repeated Osric, demanding, if not reassurance, then at least finality.

Torgal shrugged and threw up his hands. "If we move him now he'll die. I'll work what skill I have, and we'll know in a few days. I'll do all I can, my King, but I work no miracles."

Osric grasped Torgal's hand. "We'll leave miracles to God. Cathal!"

The warrior holding Rolfe stiffened. "Yes, sire?" he said.

"Fetch Torgal's things and make camp."

"Aye!" enthused Cathal and stomped out of the cabin bellowing orders.

Unsupported, Rolfe slumped to the floor and cried out as the king approached. "I didn't know who he was, lord. I found him on the riverbank. I did him no harm!"

"Of course you didn't," Osric enthused, pulling the unfortunate man to his feet. "Rise. Dine with me tonight, and tell me your tale." He flung his arm around the trembling fellow to escort him outside when he beheld an odd if familiar sight. Perched on a stool near the door was a black and red bird. It seemed to be smiling.

———

They dined beneath a great tent where between mouthfuls of cold meat, bread and cheese, Rolfe told his king how he had found Evan MacKeth on the banks of the River Orth.

"I've a royal warrant to search for gold in these hills, but the only thing of value I've found is your poor brother. He was just lying there more dead than alive, so I brought him here and tended him as best I might. How he came to this I don't know."

"And the bird?" Osric asked.

"Now there's strange!" cried Rolfe. "The day after I found your brother that queer thing hopped through the door and sat down on my stool without so much as if you please! I tried to frighten it away, but it wouldn't be frightened, and when I swatted it with a shovel it bit the handle in two! I let it do whatever it wanted after that. I think it speaks to your poor brother, majesty, for when it squeaks or clucks or whistles, the lad stirs. An altogether queer bird, that."

Osric agreed.

In the morning the king found Torgal still attending an unmoving Evan. On the stool, the bird winked as Osric entered the cabin; a queer bird, indeed.

"What word?" Osric asked.

Torgal shrugged. "It's too early to know, my liege. He speaks through fever of dark beasts, angels and fierce battles. He mutters names. The name 'Julian' has passed his lips many times. Does that mean anything to you?"

Osric nodded. Julian Antony Vorenius, Evan's protector and the bane of Moloch's Temple. "I know the name."

Torgal continued. "He also speaks of Aine."

"My wife's sister? Very well, but what difference does any of that make? I'm interested in his health, not who he talks about."

"I have often seen this sort of thing," Torgal explained, "when someone drifts into that strange place between shadow and light. Sometimes they speak of things that trouble their spirit--of fear, longing and love, of things done and left undone."

Osric frowned. "You have a great fondness for riddles, but can't you speak plainly? What does it mean?"

"He longs for Aine."

"They barely know one another."

"That may be, but her presence might comfort him."

Osric ran his hand through his hair. "Is that all you can offer? To command such a thing would be unforgivable, but I can request her presence if you believe it may be of use."

"Who can say? It's worth a try. Have her come to Durham."

"Durham?"

"Evan's best chance lies there; if he survives the journey," Torgal responded. "Still, by the time Aine arrives the issue may have already been resolved--one way or another."

Osric decided, "Still, it might prove the proper physic. I'll send a messenger this moment."

The bird abruptly began a series of hoots, clicks and whistles that caused Evan to stir convulsively for a moment. Then with a loud squawk and a rustle of black feathers, it flew from the stool into the growing light of morning. Osric watched it soar away over the trees.

As it vanished, the king overheard soldiers in the yard talking. "Where d'ya suppose that bird is goin'?"

"Heaven knows."

Considering these words, Osric agreed that heaven had a great deal to do with the strange bird--in fact, had everything to do with it.

Despite all efforts, Evan's condition continued to deteriorate, leaving little hope that he would ever recover. Still, there were other potions to be availed, other skills to muster in Durham. To this end, two days after their arrival at Rolfe's little cabin, the king's party started again for home.

As quickly as they dared, across uneven trails, through silent forests and over snow-capped hills, they wended their way. On the second day they chanced upon the horse of the messenger who had been dispatched to Ianfeld, but there was no trace of the rider or the scroll he had carried. A cursory search was mounted, but in the end Osric was forced to continue with the unsettling knowledge that Aine Ceallaigh wasn't coming.

So at last they arrived at Durham, home of the kings and queens of Glenmara since ages out of time. As they came out of the forest onto the broad cobbled way leading to the gates of the great city, a horn heralded their arrival. Before the last echoes had drifted over the meadow and were lost in the winter forests at either hand, the call was answered from the high walls protecting the town.

Across the river plain, Durham appeared in a bristling hedge of rooftops and spires, towers and walls as it rose up to the prominence of the Sceir Naid and the palace of the king. Osric paid little attention to the scores of inhabitants that had gathered in the narrow streets to watch him ride by. Rather, his focus was drawn to the body of horsemen moving down from the city gates to meet them. When the two groups met, Osric was amazed to see Baron Brendan Ceallaigh.

"Hail, my King," the Baron said, drawing his hand over his breast. "I have come with my daughter at your bidding."

Osric stared. What new mystery now appeared? How had Lord Ceallaigh arrived in Durham in less time than it should have taken the messenger to reach him? A messenger who, at best, was now on foot. The king was about to inquire into this unexpected development when Brendan asked, "What has become of your brother, lord?"

"Attend me," Osric replied, "We shall speak of it once he is seen to." With that he spurred his horse up the hill to the palace. It would be there-- where Evan had grown up, where he had played as a boy, where he had first laid eyes on Ivrian and

Aine, whence he had fled the murderous wrath of his brother--there he would live or die. And as Osric, High King of Glenmara, went up into the seat of his power, he was glad that whatever the outcome, his lost brother was at last home.

CHAPTER II
Prayers

The great hall atop the Sceir Nead had overlooked the confluence of the rivers Gabhailin and Cuinn for many years. Part of a much older structure, the walls of heavy stone and massive wooden pillars were carved with the runes of Olcan Aonagan, the first king of Glenmara who had reigned nearly three hundred years before.

Many events, deeds and councils had transpired in that dark, drafty chamber, but few so strange as that which took place when Osric met with Brendan Ceallaigh. Although not a hostile meeting, it was rife with tension and the unpredictable current of frustration. The necessary pleasantries were followed with hard, disturbing questions.

"You've imprisoned the man?" queried Osric.

Osric's Seneschal, Eochad, answered. "Aye, lord. It seemed the prudent thing with your majesty gone and the Baron's men hot after blood."

Brendan snarled, "I can control my men, but I would fain know why your messenger steals into my daughter's bedchamber and leaves this behind?" He held up a parchment scroll affixed with the broken seal of the Family Murchadha.

Osric waved his hands as if to clear away the haze of confusion that had filled the room. "You'll have an explanation as soon as I have one. Eochad, who have you imprisoned?"

"Ruarc of Finegal, my lord."

Osric leaned forward in his great chair. "That's the messenger I sent. And you found that man in the private chambers of your daughter?"

Brendan shook his head. "No, majesty, but the scroll was discovered on the child's bed. She brought it to me and here I am. Your man admitted he carried the message."

"To your castle? To you?"

Brendan shook his head with greater agitation. "The man speaks with the tongue of fools. He claims he never delivered it, but here it is."

"Yet seven days ago Ruarc was with me fifty miles north of Eonacht." Osric declared.

"And yesterday, Ruarc wandered into the palace suffering from a blow to the head," interjected Eochad.

"Seven days ago my daughter brought me the scroll," puzzled Brendan. "We came straight away, but we've been six days on the road."

"It appears you received the message on the same day I wrote it," Osric mused, "I can scarcely countenance such a thing, yet there it is. What does Aine say?"

"She speaks of dreams."

"Dreams of a black and scarlet bird, no doubt."

"How does my lord know that?

"I'm king, aren't I?" Osric said with a smile. "I'm required to know. Eochad, send for Aine Ceallaigh. I would hear what she has to say."

But Aine could not be found.

———————

Though Aine Ceallaigh remained unaware of the contents of the parchment scroll she had discovered on her pillow, she recognized the importance of any document set with the royal seal of the House Murchadha. Vexed by such an unforeseen event, her father had ordered the castle searched, but finding no intruders, he had questioned Aine at length. Yet all she could offer was the remembrance of a strange bird. Dismissing such stories out of hand, Brendan turned his attention to preparations for the journey to Durham

The trip was cold and exhausting, and they arrived at the great city in the dead of a sullen, starless night. Finding Osric away, Aine's father had demanded answers from the King's Seneschal while Aine remained in her chambers.

Now, pacing the marble floor, her heart mimicked the fire dancing in the hearth as she recalled the single word the bird had spoken: *"Evan."* In the end she was certain there would be a simple explanation for the mystery, that the scroll was just a scroll and the dream just a dream. After all, it wasn't odd that she dream of Evan; she had done so since childhood. After their unexpected reunion some weeks past, why shouldn't she think of him quietly in her sleep?

"Evan," she said, trying to capture the sound as she remembered it, and she laughed because she couldn't sound like a talking bird. Who indeed might?

"Evan," she said once more, and her anticipation soared. She longed to see him without chains or iron bars to stand between, without the greater barrier of his bitter heart.

Yet with all he had suffered, who could blame him? Still, everything was different now. A remarkable transformation had taken place across the whole of Glenmara since High King Osric had given his life to Iosa Christus.

Not the least of these changes had been the transformation of Moloch's Temple into the Church of the One True God. Just outside the chamber window, the massive spires of a new Cathedral rose against the background of the winter sky. In the span of a few short years the Glory of Iosa Christus had shaken the power of the Priesthood, and even the air seemed sweeter for it.

Aine was still in the midst of this reverie when an insistent scratching drew her attention to the door. She stomped her feet and said, "Shoo! Shoo!" to discourage whatever rodent had disturbed her privacy, but the scratching continued. At length, prepared to do battle, she flung open the door.

"Begone!" she cried, and then found herself speechless. There in the corridor, peering up at her with large, unblinking eyes, was the bird. It smiled—impossible for a bird—and spoke a familiar word: "Evan." Before Aine could recover from the rush of excitement, the bird raced away. The girl ran after, but soon the only sign of the creature was the steady *click, click, click* of its talons echoing through the chill air of the corridor. "Wait!" she entreated, but the bird didn't heed.

The sounds soon faded altogether, replaced by the scraping of Aine's slippered feet against the rough stone floor. With the bird nowhere in sight, she found herself at the foot of the broad steps leading up into Torgal's Tower--Torgal Umliath, Torgal the Terrible.

Torgal was mysterious and ancient, renowned for his foul temper especially where inquisitive youngsters were concerned. It was widely believed that this spiteful old man had turned numerous children into a tragic menagerie of bats, reptiles and hedgehogs, so Aine had no desire to stumble upon him in the dark confines of his shadowed domain. As she turned to renew her search for the bird, something stumbled into her.

In point of fact, something hurtled into her headlong, throwing her to the unyielding hallway floor. There followed a great clatter, a resounding crash of shattering glass and a despairing voice: "Oh no! He'll have my head! My head!"

Aine rolled over to find her gown covered in broken glass and smeared with unctuous, yellow paste. She returned angrily, "Your head should be forfeit for hurling honest people down like ninepins. You've ruined my gown!"

On the floor beside her, a boy of about her own age surveyed the scene with tearful brown eyes, his dull brown hair matted with whatever substance had been in the now shattered jars he had been carrying. Tied about his narrow waist was an apron stained with what appeared to be blood. The boy shook his head. "I must get back to the apothecary! This ointment was for Master Torgal, for the brother of the king! They'll have my head!" He leapt up, but Aine grabbed his arm before he could get away.

"What of the king's brother?" she asked.

The boy tried to pull free, but the dainty little girl slammed him into the wall, and he threw up his hands in surrender. "I'm sorry about your dress," he offered, hoping to quench the dangerous lights flashing in her eyes, "but I must go!"

"What of the king's brother?" she demanded, her hand twisting at the boy's tunic.

"He lies dying in the tower!" he said. The strange, angry girl released him and ran up the tower stair several steps at a time. The boy went back to his mission.

Urged on by fear, Aine ran faster than was prudent in a long dress. Evan dying? How was that possible when only a short time ago she had seen him strong and hale? Was the vision of this red and black bird merely a harbinger of Evan's death? If so, the dream was become a monstrous nightmare.

Above her the bright glow of torches beckoned, so she staggered up and up past the light until she emerged into a large room. There in the shadow, a dim figure blocked her way. "Who are you?" the figure growled. "Get ye hence or I'll fashion you into a rock!"

"You will not, Master Torgal!" Aine snapped. "Nor shall you threaten me. I've come to see Evan."

"The High King himself does not venture here unbidden, much less some--girl!" bristled Torgal, "Who are you?"

This tactic failed to produce apologetic submission. "I am Aine Ceallaigh," she declared, "daughter of Lord Brendan Ceallaigh, sister to Queen Ivrian who walks where she will in this kingdom, even into this tottering tower without your leave, great sir. Your clumsy apprentice told me the king's brother is sorely wounded. Where is he?"

Torgal's wrinkled face twisted into a smile. So this was Aine. "Peace then good lady, you shall see him. But he is fiercely wounded, grievously ill."

"How?" she asked as tears welled in her eyes.

Torgal shook his head. "Who can say? He has spoken but little since he was found on the banks of the Orth. Yet from his darkness he has spoken your name many times."

"My name?"

"Your name. So the king sent for you. But how have you arrived so soon? No messenger could have reached you in so short a while."

"The king's scroll," she said, "The bird *did* bring it, famous creature, he!"

"Bird? Do you speak of a cunning thing, black and red as large as this?" asked Torgal, holding out his hands to approximate the size.

"The same! I saw him but moments ago."

"He is attending Evan now. Come, I will take you to our patient."

Torgal escorted Aine past a jumble of tables cluttered with strange gadgets, piles of dusty books and glassware full of colored liquids. Beside an embroidered curtain he paused and looked into her startling blue eyes to gravely say, "He may die in spite of all I can do, but he may take comfort in your presence. Go to him. You may be his best, last hope."

Together they drew back the curtain and went in.

———

"Where is Aine?" grumbled Brendan, angrier than ever. "It's just like her to go wandering about when others may be inconvenienced! But I may as soon be blunt, my lord; I don't like any of this.

Messages delivered into my child's bedchamber, strange flying creatures, and now you request that Aine attend your sick brother. Forgive me, majesty, but I don't like the boy. If you had heard the things he said about you..."

"There is little he could have said that wouldn't be true," Osric returned impatiently. "Do you refuse me? Will you not send your daughter to Evan?"

From the edge of his vision, Brendan saw the look in Ivrian's eyes. It was one thing to disappoint the High King; it was quite another to provoke the Queen, especially when she was your daughter. Brendan shook his head in resignation. "I'll not refuse you."

Osric summoned Eochad to command, "Set the servants to find Lady Aine. We shall go to my brother."

The party had reached a sharp, shadowed turn in the corridor when someone careened off of Brendan and crashed to the floor. Before the figure could stir, the Baron was prodding it with the point of his sword. "What mischief?"

"What mischief?" cried a small voice. "Who's in my way now?"

Brendan prodded harder. "Who are you addressing? I, who would as soon skewer you as see your insolent face, or the King and Queen?"

29

A youthful face peered up from the shadows only to cower again at the sight of the fierce warrior and the High Monarchs of Glenmara. The boy covered his head with his arms. "Mercy, great lord," he wailed, "I was hurrying to get these medicines to your poor brother!"

The King scolded, "Your haste has served you ill this day."

"It's truth," whined the boy. "Twice now I have been undone in my errand for Master Torgal. I'll be hanged!"

Brendan added sourly, "If there is justice. Who else have you assaulted today?"

The boy huddled closer to the floor. "It wasn't my fault! That wild girl came from nowhere and ruined everything. She shoved me into the wall!"

"Aine?" suggested Brendan.

"And where did this wild girl go?" Ivrian asked gently.

"To Master Torgal's tower, sweet lady. Forgive a clumsy fool, Your Majesties..."

But when he looked up, the lad found himself alone. Nearly in despair, he set about his task a third time.

The enclosure was small and drab, furnished with a single chair, a small table covered with medicines and a plain wooden bed. Perched upon the foot of this bed, gripping the railing with long, black talons, was the bird. It winked as Aine entered the room, but the girl hardly noticed, for on the bed lay Evan.

He was more pale than the sweat-damp linens that clung to him. A bloodstained bandage swathed one shoulder, but even the careful wrapping couldn't hide the red, distended flesh that stood out in violent contrast to the shade of the surrounding skin. The handsome face was pinched and drawn, wax-like and still.

Aine pulled away from Torgal, a lump rising in her throat. *He is dead*, she thought as she stepped to the bedside, *and I am too late*. "Oh, Evan," she whispered, "what has become of ye?" She pressed his cold, lifeless hand against her cheek. "Is there nothing to be done?"

The old man sighed. "I have done all I can. Only pray now, child. He is in God's Hands."

Together, the unlikely pair raised their spirits in prayer. And the strange bird smiled.

When the king's party arrived, Aine offered her hand to Ivrian who offered hers to Osric, and soon they had ringed the bed with their bodies and their supplication. The strange bird smiled more broadly, shifted its feet and made an odd assortment of bird noises.

"What do you want?" demanded Evan, though none but the bird could hear him.

"Wake up. You've been asleep long enough. Many visitors have gathered round you."

Evan frowned. Had anyone else in the room been watching, they would have noticed his mouth twitch. *"Go away, wretched bird. I'm dying, and right comforting it is, too."*

"You're just lazy! I didn't fly all over creation delivering scrolls and fetching people to your bedside just to watch you die. Iosa has plans for you."

"How would you know? He hasn't mentioned it to me!" complained Evan.

"You haven't been listening! He's been talking but you're ignoring Him. Wake up!"

"I will not!"

"Open your eyes or I'll bite you!" warned the bird and leapt onto the bed.

Now it happened that although no one in the room could hear Evan speaking to the bird, everyone could hear the bird. It squawked and chirped with increasing fervor until those praying could scarcely concentrate. Moreover, Osric thought it inappropriate for such a raucous serenade to accompany Evan's death. The king looked up just as the creature bounced onto Evan's chest.

"Here then, wild bird! Get ye hence!" Osric demanded and made to brush it off the bed.

For its part, the black and crimson creature rounded on the king and hissed so fiercely that everyone drew back in surprise. Brendan drew his sword. "Stand back and I'll kill it. It is possessed of demons!"

"It is not!" insisted Evan. Turning back to him they saw his eyes were open.

Aine brushed Evan's hand with her lips. "Stout lad," she said, weeping.

In turn, Evan reveled in Aine's beauty. He had dreamt of her in dark places, had seen her girlish, freckled face framed in sunlight hair, and seeing her now, feeling her squeeze his hand, was a great joy.

The wounded boy looked at those gathered around him and at the Watcher sitting on his chest. His Watcher. Julian. Evan gave a weak smile. "Now," said the bird with a satisfied smirk, "isn't that better?"

Evan weakly replied, "Perhaps. But get off me, you great, heavy thing before you do me a mischief."

Julian hopped back onto the bedpost.

Aine marveled, "It understands you?"

"Yes."

She wanted to ask more questions but Osric laid a hand on Evan's forehead. "My prayers have been answered," he said quietly. "You've come back to us with many unanswered questions and an altogether odd pet, but you're home now."

"The bird's name is Julian," whispered Evan and then he was asleep.

Osric embraced his wife and then approached Torgal, who was closely inspecting his patient. "Choose a reward," said the king. "Any honor, any treasure is yours but for asking. You've saved him."

Torgal shook his head. "I'm skilled in the way of healing, but nothing I did caused this. Look at him. Color is returning to his face while five minutes ago he was so near death that it was a matter of grave doubt that he lived at all. I didn't save him; 'twas the Lord God of Hosts."

Osric replied, "Nonetheless, I shan't forget your efforts, brave Torgal."

They were taking their leave when a horrendous crash shattered the moment, filling the room with the echoes of breaking crockery and falling furniture.

On the floor in the adjoining room, tangled amidst the legs of a small table, the remnants of a chair, and countless items of broken glass, lay the unfortunate surgeon's apprentice. He saw Torgal, the King and Queen, the horrible man with the sword and that awful girl. Then he laid his head on the cold stone floor and wept.

CHAPTER III
Visions

It was spring in Glenmara. The last snows of winter had gone to swell the rivers, leaving only the high peaks of the mountains mantled in frosty white. Across the country the landscape renewed itself with explosions of green and yellow, orange and blue, scarlet and vermilion as trees and bushes burst forth with new growth. Millions of wildflowers carpeted the hills and meadows. It was a time of renewal that carried the promise of new life and the wonders of Spring Festival.

From time before memory the people of Glenmara had celebrated the seventh day of May with a display of parades, feasts and a fabulous public market where travelers from far and wide came to buy and sell everything from livestock to silk, jewelry to tools, medicines to spices. There were magnificent contests too, including the Grand Tournament.

Springtime in Glenmara heralded celebration in many quarters. Every village had its own version of Spring Festival, while larger cities like Eonacht held spectacles that in many ways overshadowed the events that would occur in the capital city of Durham. But though Eonacht's festival was highly regarded and widely attended, no tournament was held there.

Since the days of King Aonagan, the Grand Tournament had always been held in Durham. Notwithstanding the bribes and political maneuvering directed toward moving the entire affair to Eonacht, the tradition of centuries wasn't easily changed.

Knights and men at arms from all over the kingdom traveled to Durham at festival time. Often warriors from distant lands with fantastic armor and strange weapons journeyed to the games to compete for trophies, gold and glory.

It was the middle of April now, and the preparations in Durham had reached a frantic crescendo. Carpenters worked from first light until well after sunset, continuing with lanterns and torches. Spreading south across the meadow, a rapidly growing forest of pavilions rose from the sward, splashing the landscape with brightly painted cloth and magnificent flags. The whole of the acreage between the banks of the rivers

Gabhailin and Cuinn overflowed with people who milled about like so many ants. It seemed impossible that anything remotely resembling order would ever come from the chaos at every hand, but slowly the fair grounds began to take shape.

It was a wonderful time to be alive. The air itself was charged with excitement and anticipation as the Festival drew near. Yet there was one who felt neither excitement nor anticipation in any of the activities pertaining to the coming celebration. Indeed, it seemed that the future held very little for this sad figure. In the glory of his youth with the wide world at his feet and every possibility open to him, Evan MacKeth lay stricken by his wounds.

Years before when he had fled the palace, Evan had intended to return only to kill Osric and take Ivrian Ceallaigh for his own. He couldn't have imagined he would someday be reconciled with his brother or that his entire life would be forever changed by the mercy of Iosa Christus. But of all the things he could not have foreseen, the most unexpected was his present state.

"Raise your arm," Torgal ordered.

Obediently, Evan raised his right arm over his head and held it there for a few trembling seconds before letting it drop. He grunted.

"Now the other," Torgal intoned.

The patient looked down at his left arm as if willing it to rise while the muscles in his neck and shoulder bulged in painful protest. Yet the arm moved only a few inches before flopping back against his side.

"Again," Torgal insisted.

"Leave me alone, can't you?" Evan snarled, "What's the use?"

"Nothing will change if you don't try."

"Nothing will change if I do! It's been months and I'm still as weak as an infant!"

"Then I suggest you concentrate on your limbs instead of self-pity."

"What do you know about it? Nothing you've done is any good! I can barely walk."

"That's right," Torgal enjoined, "nothing I did brought you back from the brink of death; it was God's Grace that saved you and you're throwing it back in His face."

"Don't preach to me, old man! Leave me alone, can't you?" Evan snarled, "Get out!"

Torgal bowed and departed.

Evan slumped back in the settee, anger ebbing into exhaustion. Torgal was right, but that didn't make the truth any more palatable. The pain seemed the only constant for his future--that and the promise it would worsen as he aged.

Yet worse than any physical ailment, the turmoil in his spirit weighed upon him both asleep and awake. From every direction, a bitter despair clutched at him until he could scarcely breathe from the cruel thoughts that stampeded through his mind.

What should have brought joy taunted him with a constant reminder of his uselessness. Better he had died in Westerfeld than end as a cripple. Better he had never met Aine than to long for what he could never attain.

Thoughts of his brother tormented him too. Though Osric was a changed man, there remained between them a wound every bit as devastating as anything possible in the physical plane.

If his mentor had been present Evan might have felt more at ease. Julian Antony Vorenius was wise in the ways of the world, kind, forbearing and strong. He had taught Evan everything the young man knew of worth, saved him from the Priests and brought him the witness of Iosa Christus. But Evan had thrown all that away, had denied the man for his own selfish, destructive desires. Now Julian was gone, perhaps forever.

None of this calculated the effect the bird was having on Evan's mood. It delighted in antagonizing him, and like Torgal, displayed no compassion whatever. Evan was still contemplating the obnoxious creature when it flew through the window and landed on the table.

"I was just thinking about you," Evan grumbled.

Julian bobbed his head. "Good thoughts, I trust."

"I'd rather not say," Evan replied.

"Oh come now! I'm the best thing that's ever happened to you, though I can't say the reverse is true."

"There you go again! I thought you were an Angel. Angels shouldn't be so awful."

"Perhaps you're right," Julian clucked, "but how should I respond when you're so gloomy all the time?"

Unwilling to be criticized by a bird, Angel or not, Evan changed the subject. "Where did you live when you were a bird?"

"What do you mean? I'm still a bird whether here or there," scowled Julian.

"No, I mean before you were my Watcher. What was your life like before?"

The bird sighed. "Simpler. I lived in a great tree many days' flight from here. The trees here are but saplings by comparison. In the dark forests I hunted and soared above the world of land-bound things. I saw very few of your kind and kept well away from those I did. They are quite unpredictable."

"My kind?" mused Evan.

"Yes. Your word for them is 'human,' I believe."

"What's your word for them?"

Julian laughed. "You can't translate it into Common Language; you can't translate any of my language into human speech."

"How can that be? We're talking now and I understand you very well."

"Foolish Boy! Even I, the wisest of birds, can't explain why I'm here talking to you when I should be in the forests of my hatching. Only The One True God can answer such questions. He's a very fine translator."

Evan frowned and pulled his useless arm into his lap. "I wish He'd translate more clearly. How can I be a Warrior of the Son if I'm crippled? There's been a dreadful mistake."

"Don't you believe in Iosa's wisdom?" scolded the bird. "Doesn't He know what's best? It's in Scripture, you know. *All things work together for the good for those who are called together according to His purpose.* Why forget that now?"

"Because this isn't what I imagined!" raged the boy. "I was prepared to die for Him, but not for this!"

"Stop complaining." Julian admonished. "God knows what He's doing."

"But what am I supposed to do?"

"Each day do something for someone who cannot repay you?" offered the bird.

"Where did you hear that? My teacher used to say that all the time."

"I know. I read your mind, although there's not much to read."

Evan ignored the insult. "Well, it's useless information anyway. How can I do anything for anyone?"

"Time will tell. Surely there must be something you can do; you're a Warrior of the Son."

"If Julian were here, he'd know."

"I am here!" the bird retorted.

"Not you, your namesake, Julian Antony Vorenius. He's been a Warrior of the Son for decades."

"Didn't he tell you anything?"

"He told me lots of things, but none of them seem to apply to this circumstance. I haven't any answers."

"There's me," the bird offered.

"Yes. You're an Angel. Shouldn't you be able to tell me something?"

Julian shrugged. "With Iosa's help, we can find the answers—even if you are a Foolish Boy."

Evan mumbled crossly, "You needn't be so rude. I'm not as foolish as all that."

"Well," said the bird, hopping up beside Evan, "at least you like birds. Not so foolish."

"I've often wondered why you weren't a lizard."

"Bah! I eat lizards. Very tasty!"

"You've grown rather fond of other meat-- lamb in particular. I fear for the flocks of Glenmara."

"Sheep are good," Julian agreed, "but not raw. Cooked is better."

Evan shook his head and smiled. Eventually Julian always made him smile. "You're unlike any bird I've ever seen, talking or not. Are there many of your kind?"

"No. It's hard to find mates. I'll never find a mate here. Poor Julian," moaned the bird, pretending to cry.

"Torgal says Cronids are quite rare," offered Evan.

Julian twisted his head to one side. "Cronids, did you say? What are Cronids?"

"You. You're a Cronid. Torgal found your picture in a book."

The bird threw back his head and strutted around the settee. "I'm not a Cronid. I'm a Zalathrax."

"Zalathrax?"

"Yes. That's what we call ourselves."

Evan scratched his head. "I thought you couldn't translate your language into human speech. *Zalathrax*?"

"I made it up," bragged Julian. "Zalathrax sounds better than Cronid, don't you think?"

Julian marched along the cushions for a moment more, pleased with things in general. It was good to be a Watcher, and there was always plenty to do. Eating prepared meals (splendid fare!), sleeping (on pillows chased with gold thread, no less!), spying out the complicated architecture of the palace, the great Cathedral and the town of Durham. There was some danger in this, for not everyone liked birds, and on several occasions he had been attacked with arrows or stones. For some unfathomable reason, humans were wont to hurt things--a curse afflicting much of mankind as evidenced by the constant warfare flaring up throughout the wide world.

It was but one of the confusing concepts that Julian faced in his new role. As a bird he had instincts, skills, knowledge, all associated with the things common to all manner of birds. As a Watcher he had none of that: all he had was a Still, Small Voice that spoke to him without words, that told him things he couldn't imagine and couldn't explain. How it had terrified him when first he heard it! And although the fear was gone, he was still uncomfortable with the circumstance.

Julian knew that Evan was also dealing with unfamiliar emotions, though the bird couldn't begin to imagine what those emotions were. Humans were incomprehensible, but the Watcher knew it was his duty to push his charge in the proper direction. So now, since the Foolish Boy had fallen asleep and Julian wasn't through talking, he pecked the boy sharply on the knee.

Evan woke with a howl. Had he been better able, he might have tried to throttle the avian menace, but as things were, he just glowered and rubbed his wounded leg. "What are you doing, fell creature?"

"Getting your attention. You sleep too much and there's much to do."

"Much to do? What am I supposed to do? I'm a cripple!"

"You whine a lot for a warrior. Aren't you supposed to be stoic? This day for the Lord!" Evan glared at the bird, who smiled in return. "Be glad, foolish boy. All is well. You'll see. When this is but a memory and things have returned to their blessed calm selves, I won't say, 'I told you so.' Rather I will bite you, Evan MacKeth, and then you will understand the wisdom of your Watcher!"

"Don't think that you can bite and peck me at your whim! When I recover I'll clip your wings!"

The Watcher laughed happily. "Recover did you say?"

"Well, I hope..."

"Hope! Hope! Foolish Boy has hope! Now add some faith to that hope and be glad. The Lord is in control." With that Julian flew away.

Evan sighed. He did have hope and faith but that seemed little enough with everything he had lost. Still, the settee was comfortable, and the morning sun was pleasantly warm. He slept.

Osric Murchadha was sick of petitions. Although it was the duty of any monarch to hear the complaints and entreaties of his subjects, it was still a trying responsibility. In theory, petitions could be brought before the king at any time, but with so many people coming to Durham from all over the kingdom, the days surrounding Spring Festival brought more than the average number of persons seeking special consideration from the final arbiter of law in Glenmara.

There were land disputes, trade disputes, disputes over inheritance and taxes. Wealthy families sought to position sons and daughters in the royal court. Young knights full of ardor came seeking dangerous quests to prove their valor and devotion to the king. An endless stream of petitioners crowded the hallways as they awaited audience with their sovereign.

Groaning, Osric leaned back in the uncomfortable throne. He had been threatening to replace the overdone piece of furniture with something more gentle to his back and bottom, but at least this way he would never grow fond of sitting on his royal backside and letting others run the kingdom. His father, Yuri, had let his own power and influence lapse into the hands of priests and advisors, causing Osric much difficulty following his death.

Threatened by Claranides, High Priest of Moloch, Osric had agreed to the arrest of Evan and his mother, a decision that had led to the death of Maeve MacKeth and Evan becoming a hunted outlaw. How he wished he had defied the priests! Though that would have caused its own set of difficulties, it would have been the courageous thing to do--the proper thing. It would have made him feel he had the right to call Evan his brother. But even now that Evan had been restored to him, even now that Osric had tried, as much as was possible to make amends for the disaster he had wrought in both their lives, the king's guilt was heartfelt.

He longed for his brother's acceptance and forgiveness though he knew he was asking too much. There was the will to reconcile, but it was too soon to completely bridge the terrible chasm between them. They had determined to leave it all in the Hands of the One True God Who would surely resolve the issue, but God worked in God's time.

Throughout the long morning the king continued his duties until, by early afternoon, there was only one individual left to see. "Who now, Eochad?" sighed Osric, relieved that he was nearly done.

Eochad looked down at the list and glanced up nervously.

"Well? Who's the last?"

The Seneschal swallowed with difficulty. "Cedric, m'lord."

"Cedric? Cedric who?"

"Cedric the Plowman," replied Eochad, throwing up his hands, "There's been a mistake. I'll send him away."

"Cedric the Plowman?"

"His name is on the list, lord, though I cannot say why."

It was unheard of for a commoner to stand before the king. The concerns of such unremarkable persons were always addressed by their immediate liege—a Warden, a knight, at most a Baron—but never by the king himself. So what was a simple plowman doing there? More to the point, who had arranged it?

"Bring him," ordered Osric, curiosity overcoming his sense of decorum.

A moment later a small, insignificant appearing man was escorted into the chamber. He was dressed in coarse woolens, which though ragged, appeared clean. In his arms he clutched a wooden box as if it contained a great treasure. Brought before the throne he dropped quickly to his knees.

Irregular, thought Osric, *but he is one of my people.* "What brings you here, Cedric the Plowman?"

Without raising his head the little man raised the box toward the king. Eochad snatched it from the plowman's hands and raised the lid.

"Seize him!" the Seneschal screamed. "Seize him!"

The guards responded violently, pummeling the now prostrate peasant with their spear butts before pinning him to the floor. Osric leapt up. "What are you doing?"

"My liege," stuttered Eochad, holding out the box. Nestled inside was a human head.

Since coming to the palace some months before, Aine had been in a constant blur of motion preparing for Spring Festival. She had sewn flags, embroidered garments, helped lay plans for the River Parade, and worked long hours decorating the cathedral for the elaborate church ceremony that would celebrate the beginning of festivities. And now, they were to have a priest all the way from Ascalon.

Once, Ascalon had been the center of the universe, her legions controlling most of the world, and though her empire had diminished, she was still rich and influential. Ascalonian ships sailed to the far-flung ports of the globe, bringing back exotic goods, strange animals and rare jewels. From the countries of the east, every trade route converged on the magnificent city of Pelakapar making the old adage "Every road leads to Ascalon" an apparent fact. Along one of these roads, Glenmara's priest was coming to Durham.

Aine's anticipation soared with each new arrival; often she would race to a turret to get a quick glimpse as travelers approached from afar. It was such a circumstance that reunited her with an old friend--or if not a friend, then at least an acquaintance. Rushing breathlessly up the stairway of the high southwest tower, she flew into someone, sending them both tumbling.

Before Aine could get up, beg pardon or draw another breath, she heard a familiar voice: "Sweet lady of misfortune, why do you seek my ruin?"

Beside her lay Martin Reamon, the late physician's assistant. "Why, Martin! Whatever are you doing with that great trumpet?"

The boy retrieved the brassbound steer horn and inspected it for damage before carefully placing it in his lap. "Since I was too clumsy to remain Master Torgal's assistant, I've been given to the Herald to see if he can make something of me." Martin helped Aine to her feet.

"Blow us a tune, then!" insisted Aine, clapping her hands with delight. "Play!"

He raised the horn to his lips, took a great breath and blew a long, low note that danced out over the town until it was swallowed up by the afternoon sky.

"Magnificent! You'll make a fine herald." Aine leaned over the parapet to catch a glimpse of the horsemen riding into the outer town. Even at such distance it was easy to identify her father and Brian Beollan among the new arrivals.

She smiled. The people she most loved would all be together: Ivrian and her father, Brian and Evan. She grabbed Martin's arm again. "Come," she said, pulling the boy toward the stair. "We'll visit the King's brother! Come!"

Reluctantly, Martin followed the girl to Evan's rooms where they found him asleep on a cushioned settee. Martin was shocked by his appearance, for lying there so pale, gaunt and still, Evan looked more dead than alive.

"Blow your horn," whispered Aine with an impish smile.

"I'll not!" protested Martin.

"Oh...," complained Aine, wrestling the horn away from him. She blew fiercely on the instrument but produced only an uneven croaking noise.

Evan opened one eye. "Was that a serenade or an attack?"

"This is Martin Reamon," laughed Aine, dragging the boy forward. "I told you about his dreadful luck with Torgal the Terrible. Now he is Chief Herald of the King's Court!"

Martin snatched back the horn. "Nay, lord," he said, "I am but a student."

Aine frowned. "Oh, Martin, you're too young to be so serious. But I have wonderful news, Evan. My father and Brian have arrived! You remember Brian, don't you?"

Evan nodded. "I remember him," he said and his eyes narrowed as he envisioned Aine wrapped in the strong arms of Brian Beollan.

"There's word of our Priest too," Aine continued. "He arrived in Eonacht last week. Eochad had it from a rider this morning."

"A priest?" asked Martin. "Beg pardon, m'lady, but might I ask what this priest looks like?"

Aine returned a quizzical look. "I've never met the man."

"It's just that I could recognize a Priest of Moloch, but a priest of the One True God? Do we know his name? Who sent him? What he's going to do once he gets here?"

"For pity's sake, Martin!" cried Aine, "You're a curious boy, but how are we supposed to know?"

Evan was curious about the priest too, but at the moment he was focused only on the girl sitting beside him. Had Martin not been present he might have tried to kiss her--anything to claim her affections before Brian stole her away. He knew it was selfish, but she meant so much to him, brightening his days with her charm and wit and eternal optimism. He had thus far made no declaration of his feelings only out of shame at his helplessness.

Meanwhile, Aine asked Martin, "Do you know the One True God?"

Martin nodded. "I've heard the name, though I don't know much about Him. I should imagine He's much like old Moloch."

Evan's attention instantly switched to Martin. "And you'd be hopelessly wrong with such a poor guess. The One True God is nothing like Moloch. Moloch is a pale and insignificant thing, a demon, a wraith, an evil abomination before my God."

Evan's voice was filled with such conviction, his eyes so aflame with passion, that Aine was overcome. His grip upon her hand grew tighter as he spoke the glory and power of Iosa, and the young girl felt an overwhelming desire to embrace him.

Often enough she had wished that he would soundly kiss her. Watching him now, so animated and expressive, so devoted to his Lord, she felt that desire redoubled. Would he never see the longing in her eyes nor detect the longing in her heart?

Martin was moved by a deep curiosity, and though this was the brother of the High King and he was nothing at all, he yet found the courage to ask, "My lord, what is different about the One True God?"

"He doesn't joy in burnt offerings and the blood of innocent children, for one."

"Then how do you sacrifice to this God?"

Evan fixed the boy with a hard stare. "He is not *this* God, He is *the* God Who made the heavens and earth and all things that were made.

He is the Father of everything, the Creator of everything."

"Everything? Did He fashion the palace?"

Evan wasn't certain whether this upstart of a boy was being impudent or ignorant. Suspecting the latter he answered, "Of course He didn't make the palace, but He made the mountains whence came these walls of stone and the trees from which this table was made and the sheep that gave us the wool for our garments. Everything around you comes from Him."

"Did he make Moloch as well?" asked Martin.

Evan's eyes widened. "Yes!" he blurted, though he wasn't certain he was correct. Did the One True God create Moloch? For that matter, did Moloch really exist at all, or was he something that lived only in the twisted minds of men desperate for something to believe in? Evan had once posed a similar question to Julian Antony Vorenius who had only laughed and made some comment about the number of angels that might bathe in a thimble. Well, how many angels could bathe in a thimble? Why would they want to bathe in a thimble anyway, and what did any of that have to do with Martin's question? "Well, that's my impression at least," Evan continued. "The One True God is mysterious."

"Which is exactly why a Priest will be so valuable," offered Aine. "Surely he will know the answers."

"Yes. Yes. The Priest," mumbled Evan, falling silent.

Aine squeezed Evan's hand. His dark, green eyes now possessed a haunted quality, perhaps the effect of the terrible wounds that had ravaged his body. Perhaps in the dark caverns of Westerfeld the unfathomable evil of the Glamorth had injured his spirit in kind with his body. Perhaps he was mad. But whatever the state of his mind, whatever the condition of his body, Aine's heart was warm and full.

Martin was beginning to feel quite uncomfortable in the presence of Lord MacKeth and Lady Ceallaigh. He looked about for some way to extricate himself from the pair who seemed to have forgotten he was even there. They were gazing at each other like two idiots! Though certain he could be executed for even having the thought, that didn't change the accuracy of his observation. He cleared his throat.

With Aine sitting next to him, touching his hand, Evan had forgotten all about the One True God or Moloch or Angels in thimbles. The beauty of the golden-haired, blue-eyed girl overwhelmed him. Every freckle on her girlish face seemed to cry out for a kiss at which thought Evan shuddered with delight. But just as he began to believe that all his dreams about Aine could somehow be fulfilled, just when it seemed he could bridge the short distance between them without even moving, so suddenly darkness passed over all his hopeless joy, wrenching his mind back into shadow.

In the darkness something moved toward them. Beyond sight, its character veiled by a formless haze, it hovered over them all, blotting out the promised sun of their future.

Aine, who moments before had been ready to melt into the arms of the young man beside her, sensed the change. Suddenly Evan was agitated and tense, looking through her as though something had appeared beyond. Aine moved closer to him, cradling his trembling hand in her own. Whatever was wrong now?

Martin cleared his throat again, startling Evan out of his trance. "I beg your pardon, m'lord," stammered Martin. "I didn't intend to disturb you."

Evan's breath hissed between his teeth as he sank back on the settee. Like the vision of the Glamorth that had taken him into the darkness of Westerfeld, he knew this sense of foreboding would lead him somewhere too, and he shuddered to think where that place might be.

"Evan," Aine said, stroking his arm, "what's wrong?"

Evan gave his companion a wan smile. "Nothing. Memories. It's alright."

Aine lowered her head. Since their reunion Evan had revealed almost nothing about his experience beneath the earth, though it was plain that whatever had occurred had been most unpleasant. She wanted to share his pain as well as his joy, but denied both, she felt helpless and small.

"Really, it's nothing," Evan lied. "Perhaps I'm just tired."

"Perhaps we should leave," Aine offered.

"No. Stay a bit longer. I didn't mean to be so gloomy."

"Is it... the Glamorth?"

Evan shuddered. "The Glamorth is dead," he asserted, "and will bother no one again." Still, he marveled that he had ever had the courage to fight the creature in the first place, and he thought it unlikely he would ever be so brave again.

"Glamorth?" Martin queried timidly.

"Martin...," warned Aine.

Evan sighed. "He might as well hear it from me. The palace is full of rumors on the subject. It was a monstrous demon, cold and dark and so full of evil it would steal your breath just to think of it."

"And you went into the mountain to kill it?"

"Yes."

"Why?"

Not long ago, being questioned in any capacity by such an unremarkable person would have angered Evan. But Martin's curiosity brought to mind endless questions once posed to Julian Antony Vorenius and the patient answers returned in kind. Besides, it was a fair enough thing to ask: why had he gone into the mountain?

The answer, of course, was simple: God had commanded him. But why? There must have been an important reason for the command, some purpose deeper than the act that had achieved the end. Apart from simple obedience, though, he had no idea why he had done it. "You're a curious boy, I'm bound," he said.

"Beg pardon, lord," Martin stammered.

"Don't apologize. Be curious or you'll never learn anything. As to an answer, my Lord commanded it. I didn't dare disobey."

Nor did Martin dare ask any more questions. Evan, however, was now the curious one. "How did you find yourself in the king's service?" he asked the boy.

"I had nowhere else to go, sire."

"As if the palace were a refuge of last resort? What do you mean?"

"My Aunt and Uncle, lord. When my parents died, they didn't want me. Had my father not once been of service to Master Eochad, I would have ended a beggar on the streets of Faltigern."

"But instead you became Master Torgal's assistant."

Martin blushed, stammered and hung his head. "Aye, lord. I'm sorry I almost killed you."

"Lady Aine is right; you are too serious," Evan smirked. "Are you happy with your new duties?"

Martin fidgeted. What sort of question was that? If he said no, would it seem ingratitude? If yes, was he being entirely honest? It wasn't that he didn't appreciate everything he had been afforded, but there was nothing exciting or interesting about polishing brass horns and laundering uniforms. Still, it was better than living on the street. "I am extremely grateful for the kindness of your household," he mumbled.

"Just answer the question," glowered Evan.

Martin averted his eyes. "Yes, lord, I am quite happy."

Evan snorted. "You're a poor liar, Martin Reamon. I need a manservant. I can't promise you much excitement, but you will still have ample opportunity to play on your clarion. What say you?"

Martin gaped. Who knew where such a thing might lead? Squire? Seneschal? Ambassador?

"My lord!" he cried, dropping to one knee, "I will serve you."

"Good. I'll send for you."

Aine beamed with unconcealed pleasure at Evan's kindness, but the brief conversation had sapped Evan's strength and his dull eyes slowly closed. Aine pulled a dazed but smiling Martin out of the room.

Moments later Evan woke to the sound of Julian returning to the room with a pilfered pear in his beak. Seeing that his visitors were gone, Evan turned to the Watcher. "I felt something," he offered.

"Was it painful?" asked the bird.

"I'm serious," insisted Evan, "Something isn't right."

"Whatever do you mean?"

"A heaviness in the air, a cold shadow hanging over us. Don't you sense it?"

"You're a Warrior of the Son," Julian reminded, "God will reveal things to you that remain hidden from most."

"How do you know that?"

"Because God reveals things to me too. He leads; follow."

"How can I follow when I don't even know which direction to turn? It's just a feeling. Maybe I'm wrong."

"Maybe you are, but God isn't wrong. If you are patient, diligent, and watchful, He will reveal His plan to you!"

"I'm still a cripple..."

"You're whining again!"

"No, that's not what I mean. I had a thought a moment ago..."

"A thought? It must be very lonely!" crowed the bird as he spit out the pear core.

"And hah, hah to you, wretched bird. But if something is going on, wouldn't another set of eyes and ears be useful? Perhaps Martin might help us."

Julian scratched his head with a wing claw. "The clumsy boy?"

"Yes, the Clumsy Boy."

"Well, if you think it's a good idea. Foolish Boy, Clumsy Boy..."

"And Wretched Bird," Evan interjected. "How can such an alliance fail?"

CHAPTER IV
The Legion

Shortly after breakfast the following morning, Aine brought Brian Beollan to Evan's room. She made polite introductions, but the pair had met before, and there was no love lost between them now. Nevertheless, they exchanged cold pleasantries.

Brian was a tall, square shouldered man, with an easy grace of movement in contrast to his size. Dark, close-cropped hair crowned his head while an untrimmed mustache overflowed his lips, making it difficult to read his facial expression. Only his eyes indicated anything of his demeanor, and they grew bright indeed when he looked at Aine.

Brian's dislike of Evan stemmed from their first meeting when he had interrupted an impromptu encounter between Lord MacKeth and Lady Ceallaigh. Now it was fueled by the attention Aine was lavishing on his rival.

What Aine found appealing in this pale, thin boy was beyond Brian's comprehension. Even the story of how he had been wounded seemed a great faerie tale, though naïve little Aine believed it. If Evan wasn't a liar, he was at least fond of spinning yarns.

"I grieve at your wounds," offered Brian. "I'd find great pleasure breaking lances with you at the tourney. I wager you'd bounce well on the green."

Evan's eyes flared. "Save your grief for your own wounds. Once I recover I'll arrange them for you."

He instantly regretted his outcry. Brian wasn't the cause of his troubles, and if he were protective of Aine who could blame him? Evan was about to apologize when Osric entered the room.

Brian bowed, Aine curtseyed and Evan tried to sit up.

"Come Brian," said Aine coldly. "We beg your leave majesty."

Once out in the hallway Aine rounded on her companion. "What cruelty to speak of the tournament! When you fell ill and couldn't go on campaign against Pictish raiders, did I remind you of the great battles you were missing? You were so despondent that I despaired of your company. Men are so valiant until they must deal with their own frailty!"

"But...," began Brian.

"Speak of it no more! Go away until you've regained your senses!"

She turned and left him there, dazed, confused, and smarting. After a moment Brian wandered away shaking his head.

Aine, on the other hand, stormed back into Evan's room, interrupting his conversation with the King. "Evan MacKeth!" she cried. "How dare you threaten my friends just because you're feeling sorry for yourself! I won't stand for it do you hear? Until you stop sulking I'll have nothing more to do with you!"

An uneasy silence followed the echoes of the slamming door. Evan grimaced and ran his hand over his face. "Disaster," he said.

"Tempests pass," offered Osric.

"Leaving destruction in their wake."

Osric chuckled. "Don't be so melodramatic! I've come to invite you to a banquet tonight. It will be a grand affair. Some of your old friends will be there: Aelfric, Eowulf and Guthrum."

"The Fitzwarrens?" muttered Evan. "That's hardly an enticement. The last time I saw Eowulf I broke his nose for vexing Ivrian."

"And what a blow it was! But there will be many others there too; even the Tempest will attend. I'll wager you haven't been to such an affair since..." Osric's voice trailed off awkwardly.

"Since Father's birthday, what was it, four years ago?"

The King lowered his head as though the sudden onrush of incriminating thoughts made it too heavy to hold upright. And though Evan's words hadn't been intended as reproach, Osric's reaction filled his memory with everything that had once come between him and his brother.

"It doesn't matter now," Evan offered.

Osric tried to smile. "Of course it matters."

"No it doesn't, but there's something wrong."

"Of course. All manner of things are wrong. It will take time."

"That's not what I mean. It's something else. Something's coming. Something unpleasant."

"Whatever are you talking about?"

"You think I'm mad, don't you? Everyone does."

"No one thinks you mad. A bit odd perhaps, but after all you've been through, you've earned a little eccentricity."

"I'm not as I once was," Evan asserted. "I see things, feel things that even I don't understand. But they're visions from God, not eccentricities."

"Of course, of course. But if you don't understand, how can you expect anyone else to?"

"You don't believe me."

Osric sighed, shrugged. "I believe in the One True God Who brought us back together. He deals with each of us according to His plan, and we must trust in that."

"Then trust that something bad is going to happen."

"It already has," Osric confessed. "Yesterday afternoon I received a gift from Claranides—the head of Sir Rainault O'Guinn in a box."

"That's bad enough. What does it mean?"

"It means the power of Moloch remains. It means that despite my attempts to destroy that faith, it still holds sway over much of the kingdom," Osric continued his explanation. "When I drove the Priests out of Glenmara, most of them fled to the Hinnom Valley. Sir Rainault was tasked with arresting those remaining. But, as you can see, they're still among us."

"What will you do?"

"March on the Hinnom Valley. Glenmara will never be rid of Claranides until the High Temple is thrown down and every priest put to the sword. But such things take time and money. Soon."

"And when you go, I will ride beside you," Evan declared. "Claranides has much to answer for, and he shall answer to me."

"Good! Good! I shall depend on it. But tonight you will attend the banquet. Did you know there's a fellow here all the way from Varangia?"

"I've never met anyone from Varangia, except for Lady Fitzwarren."

"Indeed. She and this fellow Anwend Halfdane were acquainted."

"Strange he would come all this way. Lady Fitzwarren has been dead since we were boys."

"Perhaps he's here for the tournament. At any rate, you'll meet him tonight."

When Osric was gone Evan reflected on the conversation. Heads in boxes were awful things, but he didn't think that had anything to do with the unease that was gnawing at him. It was something else, something no one could see or sense or imagine, and unless he could uncover it, they would all suffer.

Julian, who had all this while been listening from a nearby chair, leapt onto the settee. "An ill wind blows," Evan said.

"I'm a bird," Julian answered. "Even an ill wind will lift me up. The Lord of Hosts will lift you up too. He'll reveal the answers, and I'll stay close to make certain you don't get into trouble."

"You're the biggest trouble I've run into since the Glamorth," laughed Evan.

"That trouble is only beginning," chirped the Watcher as he did a funny little dance. "I'll be watching you tonight. Save some roast pig for me, won't you?"

"Come with me. Sit beside me at table and you shall have your fill of roast pig."

"Indeed? I've never been to a banquet before, unless you count that one spring in the forest when there were so many frogs! What a feast that was!"

"Well, there may not be any frogs tonight, but there will be plenty of roast pig."

"What adventure!"

"It will hardly be that."

"One never knows," cried Julian, and he leapt up and disappeared through the open window.

Evan smiled. How strange his life had become! Talking to a bird didn't seem at all odd to him, though he could scarcely imagine what others thought about it. How Julian Antony Vorenius would laugh! *"An Angel? You startle me!"* he would say, or something of similar wit, and now Evan found it difficult to believe he had doubted anything that remarkable man had ever uttered. And so, as much because he trusted Julian Antony Vorenius as that he trusted the One True God, Evan lifted his spirit in prayer.

"You have brought me to this place mighty Lord. Command and I will follow." He raised his one good arm toward the sky. "In You I will place my trust."

Prayer always brought him peace, but no sooner had that peace begun to manifest itself than it was shattered by a vision of such horrid clarity that Evan shrank back in the chair to escape it.

He found himself back atop the blood-covered stairs in Westerfeld where from the shadows the hideous face of the Red Goblin Klabaga emerged. Evan had forgotten that moment, but now the memory surged back even as the scene began to change. Now Klabaga stood beneath the blue and white shade of mountains, surrounded by hundreds of Grey Goblins. In the distance, a large body of water glistened in shimmers of sunlight.

The goblins crouched among the brush and rocks beneath a stand of forest trees. They were watching, straining to see something in the direction of the lake. Evan didn't recognize the geography; it was as though he were looking at a framed picture, beyond the edges of which lay only shadow. The boy knew little about goblins either Red or Grey, but he did know they didn't like sunlight, so what were they doing above ground? He was still trying to sort it all out when Klabaga turned toward him, snarled and vanished.

Evan's pulse raced. The pieces of a great puzzle were beginning to reveal themselves, but most of the picture remained hidden in ominous shadow.

———————

Klabaga, Red Goblin of the Clan Modragu was lost in an ambiguity of emotion. He was at once elated and downcast, filled with evil glee and consumed with rage, and there was adequate reason for all of these things.

He had come far to be there. It had been an arduous journey from the caverns of his ancestors to this tree-covered mountainside, dragging all those pitiful Grey Goblins behind him. The bones of more than fifty of the useless things littered the long way from Westerfeld to the hills above Clon Miarth where they now stood. He himself had killed three, while others had fallen prey to predatory rock spiders, burrowing Oronax and bottomless, unseen pits. Then there had been at least twenty killed by the human boy Evan MacKeth. A few more had deserted, but Klabaga had gotten the remainder all the way to the cavern of Ugrik, Lord of the Northern Realm, Ruler of the Clan Drekar.

The Clan Drekar was a powerful confederation of four separate tribes brought together by Ugrik's cunning and strength. Not since the Demon War had goblins managed to put aside their quarrels and unite, even though this alliance had been accomplished at the point of a sword. Now with the help of the Glamorth, Ugrik was gathering a great army to strike at the world of men, and Klabaga had followed the call too.

When the War Chiefs of the Drekar learned of the Glamorth's death, a heated discussion had followed. Many wondered if it was possible to go on, but Ugrik was glad to be rid of the horrible creature. Nearly eight thousand warriors had flocked to his banner because of that dark beast, and now Ugrik alone commanded them.

In the end the rest had submitted to Ugrik's will, and since the presence of a Red Goblin was widely held as a good omen, Klabaga was made a war-chief and given command of the troops he had brought with him. Once Klabaga's soldiers had been quartered and fed, Ugrik summoned his new commander. "What're ya doin here?" he demanded.

Klabaga scrutinized Ugrik. He was a "dark grey," his skin almost black in contrast to the more common "light grey", but his bright crimson eyes and an angry red scar that snaked across his scowling face were the most notable things about him. "I came ta fight," Klabaga said simply.

"With Greys? Why does yer want ta fight with Greys?"

It was a fair question. "I don't," Klabaga snorted, "but I'm the last of my clan."

"And what become of yer clan then?"

"Human men came. There was a fight. I'm all what's left."

"Run away did ya?" chuckled Ugrik.

"I was a child," Klabaga countered, "not a year old."

"A babe? How'd yer survive?"

"Glandihoo."

Ugrik hesitated. Glandihoo? The legendary goblin shaman that lived beneath the Crystal Halls of Doryleaum? "What does yer know of Glandihoo?"

"He found me, was me da, cruel and heartless as he were. He taught me."

"Glandihoo? What'd he ever teach the likes of you?"

"Ta fight, ta plan, ta kill human men. That's why I'm here: ta kill human men."

"So ya come all this way ta serve with me, did ya?"

"No. I don't care nothin about ya," said Klabaga evenly. "But if'n yer goin' after human men, I wants ta go too."

"Then do as yer told and keep yer mouth shut," Ugrik threatened, "else yer'll find yerself dead. Understand?"

Klabaga nodded though his eyes spoke a quiet rage. He hated Ugrik, the same as he hated all Grey Goblins, but there was little he wouldn't suffer to bring ruin to the world of men. He submitted to Ugrik's will.

Under the tutelage of Greebo, an enormous goblin, who filed his teeth to needle points, Klabaga learned the art of warfare above ground, and in whose company he first laid eyes on the man-city of Gwenferew.

"Time ta go," Greebo ordered one day.

"Go where?" Klabaga snarled. He was tired and hungry and in no mood to listen to anything Greebo had to say. Since his arrival he had scarcely had time for anything but work as he struggled to turn his raw troops into disciplined warriors. He wanted sleep and food, but it appeared he would get neither.

"Jest follow me," Greebo insisted, "and bring yer weapons."

Klabaga snatched up his sword belt and stalked after.

Through the maze of passages and chambers that made up the dominion of the Clan Drekar, they wended their way until they arrived at a great opening in the cavern face. Here, gathered beside a fire kindled in a ring of stones, a small knot of others grumbled greetings at their approach. Greebo hardly acknowledged their presence, instead taking up a torch and proceeding past the ring of light through the fissure, down and down toward the unknown depths. Klabaga followed and glancing back discerned that most of the others had joined the procession too.

For hours they continued their silent, solemn march through the shadowed underworld. The geography of dusty black rock was unremarkable, devoid of life, the atmosphere oppressive as if somehow lacking air. How unlike the caverns of his youth, the vaulting chambers, the sculpted pillars and dark crystal of Dorylaeum! He longed for the comforting odor of sulphur, and water that tasted of iron, but Glandihoo had forced him onto this path, and there was no turning back.

The little group arrived at a sheer wall of fractured stone. Without pause or comment, the Grey Goblins began to climb, swiftly, surely ascending the carapace on shallow steps scoured out of the rock. Up and up they wound their way, death never more distant than a stumbling step or a moment's distraction, through a small opening high above the floor and into a gallery filled with bat droppings. The smell brought a stir of dim memories.

Before Glandihoo, before the Crystal Halls of Dorylaeum, before human men had come and destroyed his clan, there had been the smell of bats. Bats. He could hear them fluttering overhead like whispers from his past.

A strange sort of light insinuated itself into the chamber, growing more insistent as they approached a grotto of battered, broken stalactites hanging from the ceiling as it converged with the floor. There, beside a boulder covered with bat excrement, a narrow opening yawned out into the open sky.

The Greys squeezed through in quick succession and Klabaga followed them onto a broad platform of rock that seemed to stand at the very top of the world. Even in the darkness of night, the stunning panorama surrounding him, the uncomfortable twinkle of myriad stars overhead and the disturbing smells carried by the cool breeze, were enough to stagger the Red Goblin.

"Yer ain't never been outside afore, have yer?" laughed Greebo.

Klabaga steadied himself. "No, I ain't."

"Wait till the sun comes," Greebo warned. "It'll come from over there." He pointed with a long finger. Out over the eminence the black sky seemed to go on forever. In the distance a vast lake reflected the hideous light of the moon, and a silver-black river wound its way across the landscape like a great, gleaming serpent. Klabaga felt as though he were falling through a void, his mind struggling to process what his eyes were taking in.

"Look there," Greebo said, pointing again, "That's what we've come fer."

Down on the plain, indistinct but for a few pinpoints of light, a deeper shadow revealed itself: the man-city of Gwenferew.

"Rest now. Come dawn we'll have a better view."

The Grey Goblins chuckled, casting knowing glances at one other. They had all grown accustomed to the sunlight, but it was always pleasant to watch someone experience it for the first time. They made wagers. What would the Red Goblin do? Would he flee in terror? Become ill? Perhaps he would die; some did. But whatever his response he would have to get used to the sun if he was to lead goblins against Gwenferew. This would be his first test. The Greys relaxed and waited.

Klabaga waited too. He faced the direction Greebo had indicated and waited for the cursed sun to come. He knew it would appear from beyond the rim of the world; Glandihoo had taught him. Everything he knew about the world of goblins and men he had learned from that harsh teacher. Everything he knew about hatred came from that quarter too.

"The world of men is ruled by the sun and the moon," the shaman had told him. "Because of you, mankind will fear the dark and despair of the setting sun. But first you must understand the light. You must embrace its fearsome clarity or you will never defeat the human men."

"Where does I find it?" Klabaga asked.

"The Halls of Dorylaeum hold the beginning. Beyond that you must go above ground."

The Red Goblin shuddered. The Halls of Dorylaeum were sacred to both goblins and dwarves. The dwarves revered them for what they contained and the goblins for the symbol of what the dwarves were denied. Here Klabaga had first learned about light, and even now he hated Glandihoo for it. Deep within the dark crystal forests was a treasure so remarkable, a power so severe, that no goblin could look upon it and live; yet Klabaga had seen it, and he had not died. Now for the first time he stood beneath the dark abyss of the night sky and waited for another light that he would have to master.

The shadows began to change. They grew longer and darker as though the night had concentrated all its power in a handful of places to resist the coming brightness. The sky slowly drained itself of black. A tinge of orange slashed across the horizon. Klabaga felt his hackles rise, and sweat broke out on his forehead. The Greys watched with eager anticipation.

Klabaga saw trees and grass and the stench was suddenly thick in his nostrils. The heavy air of night gave way to the steady warmth of day and the panorama of the wide world lurched into his vision with a rush of nausea. Nothing in his experience had prepared him for these sights and smells, but when the giant red orb began to rise in the distant sky, the Red Goblin laughed to himself. Strange it may have been, disturbing and uncomfortable, but it couldn't compare to what he had seen in Dorylaeum. The sunrise paled before the Golau am Duw.

The sun was well up before any of the other goblins spoke.

"Well," growled Greebo, uncertain what Klabaga's lack of response might indicate, "have ya turned ta stone?"

Klabaga grinned. Tiny in the distance, the man-city beckoned.

"I wants a closer look," he replied. "I wants ta smell 'em."

Greebo snorted. "Well ya can't. We're ta stay here till the sun is overhead."

Klabaga shrugged. "Then lets have sommat ta eat."

The Grey Goblins exchanged questioning glances as they tried to decide who had won the wager. None of their predictions had come to pass, and suddenly they were afraid to be in the Red Goblin's presence.

After that day, Klabaga longed for a closer look at the man town. His desire for vengeance and blood bloomed into a lust that would not be sated.

So goaded on by whip and sword, Klabaga had trained his command until they staggered from exhaustion. The work was brutal and difficult, resulting in discontent and desertion, but after a few floggings and an execution, the dissension ceased.

In time he had moved his command out under the open sky to train in hidden valleys and fields. Two goblins died from the exposure before the sunlight had gone from unbearable, to tolerable, to not quite unnoticeable. By the time their training was done, Klabaga's warriors were anxious to be about the business of death.

But instead of pitched battle they had been sent on endless mountain marches, patrolling forgotten paths, scouting routes for the army. It was on one of these tedious missions that Klabaga found himself on a hillside overlooking Loch Cuinn one bright afternoon.

The sunbathed air, heavy with the smell of trees and grass, overpowered his normally keen sense of smell. The distant blue lake was bright and uninviting. Only the thought of the man-city gave him any pleasure at all, and even that was but an unfulfilled promise. Bloodshed alone could salve his passions, but Ugrik had given strict orders to avoid battle.

Just beyond the hill the terrain opened into rolling meadows of thick grass and flowers. Klabaga found it as disturbing as the distant lake, and he was glad it was nearly time to return below ground.

He was still thinking of the stew and hot gholjaka that awaited him when the wind blowing up from the lake brought the unmistakable scent of man. But it brought another, unfamiliar scent as well. Soon other goblins began to sniff the air as up the road from the lake came a group of men and horses. Klabaga had heard terrifying stories about men on horseback sweeping across the battlefield with fire and steel, and now he could imagine what terrible weapons they would be.

It was apparent that the approaching men were soldiers. Even discounting the commonality of their armor, weapons and the great red, rectangular shields they carried, it was impossible to misinterpret the precision and easy grace that even their casual march conveyed. Hidden on the edge of the bluff where the road cut into the hillside, Klabaga counted forty-three men and three horses.

"What if they finds us?" whispered Orglyx, Klabaga's second in command.

"Don't make no never mind. We're the ones whats found them. Send Glak behind them rocks and Adok ta them trees. On my signal we'll rise and take 'em."

"What about orders?" offered Klec.

Klabaga glowered at his subordinate. "Hang orders. Now do as yer told."

It took a long time for the soldiers to move up the road. They weren't paying attention to the forests or rocks around them, but Klabaga held his breath as they passed the boulders where Glak and his warriors were hidden. If that cursed Grey acted prematurely the entire ambush would be compromised. But while he was contemplating the "what-ifs," the soldiers marched right into the trap.

Yet as Klabaga was about to commence the ambush, he was overcome by the feeling that someone *had* found him. Casting about for the source of this sudden unease, a remarkable vision burst into his mind with the force of a physical blow. From a cushioned chair in a room of polished stone, the human boy Evan MacKeth was watching him.

Klabaga snarled and the picture disappeared. What mischief? He had never believed the boy was dead, but seeing him again was disturbing. Still, this unexpected interlude meant nothing; the soldiers were still going to die. Then the wind changed.

Cohm Rourke thought it grand to be a legionary of the First Century, First Cohort, Second Glenmaran Border Legion. Not that it was all skittles and beer; the work was hard, and stationed with the four Centuries at Gwenferew he had seen his share of fighting against Goth raiding parties. Still, it was better than life on his father's pig farm. He would as soon have been garrisoned closer to home where he could have maintained contact with a pretty little girl he knew, but at least he was well away from his mother who would surely skin him alive for joining the Legion if she got the chance.

The Legion offered regular meals, an ample ration of beer in the evening and a warm place to sleep each night. Life was full of promise. His Optio had put his name on a list of candidates for Signifier. Could it get better? Even though he would have to bivouac in the field again tonight and eat corn mush heated over a campfire, Cohm was well pleased.

Then, just as the wind shifted, giving them all a welcome breeze off the mountains, Cohm caught the scent of something awful. The Officer's mounts began to shy and start, and the formation came to an abrupt halt. As the Legion column split apart to escape the frantic horses, the goblins struck.

Cohm was trying to keep clear of his commander's horse when he heard a great roar from the forested slope to his right. Suddenly the hillside was swarming with hideous grey shapes that came leaping down the embankment like creatures from the pit. His mouth hanging open, legionary Rourke watched them come.

The Optio jumped clear of his unmanageable mount, bawling out orders to which the legionaries instantly responded. In seconds they presented a solid mass of overlapping shields and bristling spears.

In the first rank, Cohm held a death grip on his weapons. Even he was aware this wasn't a good place to meet a charge since the enemy had the impetus coming down the slope, but they advanced like any of the other undisciplined warrior tribes he had battled. Here was the strength of Legion training; a brawling mob of hundreds could never defeat a disciplined century of legionaries. So let the wretched things come-- whatever they were.

"They're goblins, lads," announced the Optio as he carefully checked the formation of his command, "but Legion steel will stop 'em! Stand fast to receive the enemy!"

Cohm grinned. Of course Legion steel would stop them. But what was that red creature doing?

At Klabaga's command the advancing goblins came together in an ordered formation on the hillside and launched a barrage of spears down among the legionaries.

Cohm ducked behind his shield as the air whirled with steel tipped shafts. Spears thudded quivering into shields and cries of pain punctuated the afternoon sky as missiles found their mark in flesh. Four men writhed on the bloody ground.

"Column!" roared the Optio. "To the step, forward, march!"

The Legion formation surged up the slope in a perfect alignment of shield and spear and armor. Cohm grimaced as they drew near the goblins, for worse than their stench was a closer look at them.

"Spears!" ordered Optio Zall, and the soldiers in the second rank readied themselves. "Now!"

Now the goblins received their own share of punishment, and Klabaga observed the ingenious design of the Legion spear. The spearhead was attached to the wooden shaft by a long shank of soft iron that penetrated easily and then bent: bent spears couldn't be thrown back. Three goblins fell in that first volley and it was instantly followed by a second and a third as the two lines met.

The legionaries crashed into their enemies, filling Cohm's world with struggling, cursing men and hissing, screeching goblins. Cohm stepped on a spear imbedded in a goblin shield, forced it down and thrust home with his sword. With wild elation he felt his blade pierce flesh, and the goblin crashed to the ground. Nothing could stand against the Legion!

The skill of the goblins was no match for the steady pressure of the Legion column. Klabaga signaled for Adok.

More goblins spilled out onto the road. "Refuse the left!" Optio Zall cried.

The rear rank of legionaries pivoted to cover the left flank of the column. The goblin charge staggered under the barrage of javelins, leaving a dozen casualties screaming in the dust. But the rest pressed forward.

"Rally on the roadway!" ordered Zall, and the Legion formation moved back.

They formed on the road again, and began a slow, orderly movement toward the rocks. Wounded legionaries struggled to follow since the few men that had fallen had been hacked to bloody bits where they lay.

Cohm had always found the cacophony of battle a seductive melody that stirred his ardor, but things were beginning to look grim. Often the Legion defeated much larger forces, but these goblins were disciplined fighters, and in the press of steel their greater numbers were beginning to tell. It was a struggle to hold the front line together as the full weight of the enemy pressed upon them, and although dozens of goblins had fallen, others pushed forward to fill the gaps.

But they were almost at the rocks. Zall was about to give the signal for one last desperate push that would give them time to break for the safety of the fortress-like ring of boulders when the Red Goblin gave his own signal. Suddenly a hundred more goblins swarmed up on their right.

"Refuse the right!"

As the new goblin force slammed into the unformed line, the Legion ranks fell apart. The formation disintegrated into dozens of smaller groups, and individual combats spilled out like a boiling flood all over the roadway.

The legionaries sensed defeat but there was no time to dwell on the inevitable. A few cast aside their arms to flee but were instantly cut down for their troubles. Most grew wild and grim.

Cohm threw himself into the teeming press the moment the formation collapsed, hoping to cut his way through the disorganized ranks and win free. But there were just too many goblins. There would be a few less before he was through.

Optio Zall led a handful of legionaries in a last despairing charge toward the Red Goblin, and for a moment their ferocious attack scattered all before them. But more goblins swarmed in, shouting, slashing, and mouthing a horrible droning chant of "Ulu! Ulu! Ulu!"

A spear slammed into Zall's shoulder, parted the maille and drew blood. Swords and clubs rained from all sides, stabbing and pounding, glancing from his armor and battered helmet. He was bleeding from dozens of wounds, but he slashed and clawed and kicked his way through the howling grey ranks until he reached his counterpart.

In mindless rage the Optio threw himself at the goblin commander only to fall over a wounded legionary who was trying to crawl to safety. As he struggled to regain his feet, blows falling on him from every quarter, he felt a sudden blinding pain in his back, a terrific heaviness in his chest and the very last thing Optio Zall ever saw was the awful red face of the goblin that had slaughtered his command.

Elsewhere the battle raged on, but the few legionaries remaining were wounded and impossibly beset. Cohm, down on one knee, hamstrung, knew he would never leave this battlefield, would never again see his mother or that pretty little girl. He was overwhelmed by a conflicting whirl of sadness, fear and anger.

He was sad to die in this nameless place without once more seeing home. Though only a pig farm, how he longed for the smell of the place now instead of the odor of blood and death. Cohm was afraid to die too, but above all he was angry at these terrible grey beasts that had already killed all his companions.

A blood smeared goblin loomed over him, pulling at his shield, trying to tear it from his weakening grip. Cohm swung his sword and the goblin staggered back minus several fingers. It was that singular blow that set into motion events that would profoundly affect the future of Glenmara. Cohm couldn't know it, for an instant later he was slain there on the blood-soaked road, but he had struck the most decisive blow of the battle, perhaps even of the war which was to come. No songs would men sing of Cohm Rourke, son of a pig farmer from Faltigern, but his final defiant act would provide the only hope of saving the kingdom.

It was over. The triumphant goblins chanted their battle cry, clashed sword against shield and danced among the corpses. Forty humans lay dead. Twenty-seven goblins would never again walk the world of men, while some dozen others were wounded. These made every attempt to appear unscathed, for Grey Goblins rarely assisted their own, nor carried away their wounded. Often their own companions simply killed them.

Klabaga surveyed the carnage with a perverse pleasure. This was the reason he had come, this was everything he had ever desired as far as his remembrance stretched back through the long painful years of his lonely youth. It was a good thing, a glorious beginning to the war that would utterly destroy humankind. But it wasn't yet time for celebration.

The Red Goblin posted watch and ordered the dead stripped of anything valuable. Armor, swords, shields and spears were gathered into a great pile at the base of the hill. He summoned his officers.

"We'll leave 'em a mystery," he said with an unpleasant chuckle. "We'll carry away our dead. They'll still be wondering who killed their friends when we tear down their city."

So the goblins did as they were told, and before a comforting darkness fell upon them, they had gathered up their gruesome bundles and faded into the trees. Behind they left forty human corpses, and wedged beneath a rock, three grey fingers.

CHAPTER V
Spies

The banquet hall on the Sceir Naid was alive with sound, light and the smell of remarkable food. The long, high-ceilinged room was already full of people, some seated at the massive wooden tables edging the walls, others scurrying about performing various tasks in preparation for the feast which would soon begin. In the kitchens, servants prepared a myriad of dishes to satisfy the culinary fantasies of the guests: boar, goose, venison, fish, beef, pastries, pudding, vats of soup and countless special dishes that had been requested by the numerous important visitors attending. Though elaborate, this gathering paled before the feast that would occur following the Grand Tournament. On that day even the poorest beggar, could he but get to Durham, would dine like a king. But tonight was special for a different reason.

Servants skilled in courtly protocol seated guests with special care. Such matters as place or proximity to the king's chair were delicate arrangements, so it wasn't uncommon for a slight at table, real or imagined, to lead to bloodshed. But this night, nothing had been left to chance.

Agitated and nervous, Martin arrived in Evan's chambers several hours before the festivities. With no notion of what his new duties required, he was still determined to make the most of the opportunity. He helped Evan dress while trying to avoid the ominous, unfriendly bird.

"You must calm down," Evan warned. "Only my bird bites."

Julian screeched and shook his wings.

Soon, a group of stout fellows carried Evan to the hall in a chair lashed to heavy poles. As they neared the banquet room Evan spied Brian standing in the doorway of an adjacent chamber. "Sir Beollan," he cried out, "a word with you, if I may."

Brian approached and bowed. "Your servant, sire," he returned, his eyes mocking.

Evan said, "I ask your pardon for my angry words this morning. We may never be friends, but I hope we shall not be enemies."

Brian blinked. "Perhaps I was abrupt too, m'lord."

Evan responded with a tired smile as he was carried away. *Well*, he brooded, *there's daft. Making nice with the fellow who's panting after Aine! Why did I do that?*

"Because you thought it a meet and proper thing to offer friendship to a man who has done you no ill," Julian replied.

"Reading my mind? You're an obnoxious thing," whispered Evan. He nudged the bird with his elbow.

The Watcher smiled. "I'm just trying to keep you honest, and that's no easy task."

———

The guests were seated and waiting, trading polite banter while they sipped mulled wine and nibbled at the freshly baked bread that had been piled in large platters on the tables. The room was filled with a pleasant cacophony of conversation, the clink of goblets and the clatter of musicians tuning instruments.

With a sudden punctuation of sound, a clarion announced the arrival of the king and his party. Soon the musicians played, food was brought out in dozens of courses, and the merriment continued well into the night.

Evan found the food and drink sublime, but his attention was concentrated on those gathered about him. Aine was there, of course, and it was difficult not to spend all his time staring at her. She had never looked more remarkable than that night. Her hair was twisted into one large braid that twined over her shoulder and pooled magnificently in her lap. The jade green gown, trimmed in brilliant blue and highlighted with the finest Glenmaran lace, was breathtaking. And that face! Still, she remained intent on ignoring Evan and gave him not a single glance.

To Evan's right sat Duke Fitzwarren and his sons, Aelfric, Eowulf and Guthrum. Aelfric, the eldest, was a tall, thin man close to Osric's age. An injury had long ago disfigured his face with a deep scar, marking a path across one sunken, sightless eye.

Eowulf was taller still than Aelfric, though heavier. His square-jaw was covered with a finely manicured beard of fiery red that clashed sharply with the dark black of his hair. He was an attractive man, his visage marred only by a nose that sat askew on his face, broken by a very young Evan (who now wondered if Eowulf even remembered the event).

Then there was moody, sulky Guthrum with
his soft, girlish features and the penchant for
throwing fits when he didn't get his way. He had a
beaten-down look about him, as might be expected
from any third son, but Evan remembered him as a
conniving, calculating sort who, more often than
not, got what he wanted.

Duke Fitzwarren was a balding, weather-
beaten man in his mid-forties. He was pleasant, if
aloof, speaking little and paying Evan no heed at
all. There was nothing sinister about the Fitzwarren
family, and the young Lord MacKeth turned his
attention to more promising possibilities.

At the far end of the main table sat the
Varangian, Anwend Halfdane. He was a small
man--not at all what one might expect to come out
of that land of glaciers and snow-bound fjords, of
blond-haired, blue eyed giants, the legendary
raiders of the sea—pirates, not to put too fine a
point on it. Anwend wore his coarse grey hair in
braids on either side of his harsh, emaciated face.
The man reminded Evan of a weasel with cunning,
shifty eyes partly shrouded by bushy eyebrows.
He appeared to be patiently watching, like a
creature of prey.

Evan was feeding Julian strips of boiled
mutton when the hall went suddenly quiet, and
looking up, the young man saw that Aine had left

her place at table to sit on a cushioned bench in the center of the room. She held a small lyre in her lap, and there was a flush of excitement across the white flesh of her throat.

"Lady Aine Ceallaigh will grace us with song," declared Osric with pleasure.

Aine blushed, lowered her head and ran her fingers across the lyre strings. The chord filled the hall with a startling richness and clarity, and soon the sweet song of those strings wove itself through the air in an almost tangible web of music.

Evan hadn't known Aine played the lyre, nor had he imagined the instrument could produce such a marvelous sound. But when she started to sing he could scarcely believe what he heard.

She began in a soft, clear tone that swelled to a note so high it seemed beyond the ability of any human voice. Yet more than the octave, the purity and power of the sound enchanted Evan, though not as much as the beautiful, delicate creature that possessed it. She had sung many tunes in Evan's presence, charming little ditties calculated to cheer him, but he had never heard this voice, never experienced the delirious excitement it carried, and he was suddenly jealous that anyone else was sharing in the experience. The legends of sirens luring sailors to their doom seemed entirely plausible as he listened to Aine's song.

She sang in the ancient tongue of Glenmara, little used in those days, but whose origins extended back beyond recorded history. Though a harsh, almost guttural tongue, coming from those lips, sung by that voice, it might have been the language of angels. Lady Ceallaigh painted pictures with her song beyond the mere images of the words, while her face bespoke more passion than any written verse ever could. She cast spells.

No one was immune. Even the women in the room were captivated, swept along in the overpowering current of music. Julian smiled and hummed with pleasure. But other reactions were more intense.

Evan was overcome with such longing that tears welled up in his eyes. Anwend Halfdane, more than a little in his cups, sobbed like a babe though he couldn't understand a single word the girl was singing. Brian Beollan's face was lit up in an ecstatic but entirely foolish grin. And though no one noticed, Eowulf Fitzwarren's eyes glinted with dangerous fire.

"There's a pretty biscuit," he mumbled under his breath. "A pretty biscuit, indeed."

The song went on. It was the story of Fiona, the legendary beauty whose young love had marched away to war and never returned. Hoping to guide him home, she had kept a lantern burning in her tower, high in the Balinora Mountains, and when Fiona died at nearly a hundred years of age, still the lantern burned. And in those mountains on clear mornings as the sun rose between the spires of rock known as the Towers, the light reflecting from their crystal surfaces blazed across the Hinnom Valley, Loch Aiden and all the way to Faltigern. The phenomenon was known as Fiona's Lamp.

Aine poured her heart into the song--a melody of longing and loss, eternal hope and faith in an immortal love. Thinking of proud, wonderful Evan she felt the song might have been about him and her. How she ached for his affection, but he was occupied with other things.

At the moment, however, Evan's mind was wonderfully focused. Bewitched by the song, he could think nothing of danger or darkness or his own infirmities: he was flying through a dream world where nothing bad could ever happen.

Then it was over. The final note left the audience overawed. No one spoke and some dared not breathe lest the spell of wonder surrounding them should be broken. Then the king began to applaud. Others followed suit as though waking from a wonderful dream and then, like a burst dam, the room erupted in an explosion of sound.

The hall went wild with delight. The guests clapped and stomped their feet. The men yelled until they were hoarse and pounded their fists violently on the tables. Aine curtseyed, blushed fiercely, and returned to her place.

"Well done, Lady Aine!" cried Osric. "You have captured all our hearts!"

"A pretty biscuit," Eowulf muttered through a crooked smile.

After a few moments the hall returned to some semblance of normality. The feast resumed so that for the next short while, the servants were busy filling glasses as numerous toasts were raised in honor of the young girl and her remarkable song. The musicians reluctantly took up their instruments again, hesitant to pit their ability against what they had just heard.

Then without warning, Osric stood. The musicians halted midway through a tune and the guests lay aside tankards and plates to surge to their feet in response. Evan vainly tried to rise but Osric placed a firm hand on his shoulder. "Each of you does my house honor by dining with my queen and me," he said with a mischievous glint in his eyes, "but there is one here today that I will now honor above all others, for he is my brother and this is the day of his birth! A toast, then! Drain your glasses to Evan Murchadha!"

A great roar went up as the crowd toasted Evan's health. Osric clapped his hands and brightly clad servants appeared with packages tied about with ornate ribbon. Once opened, the parcels revealed amazing treasures: a helmet chased in gold and silver runes, a shield of oak rimmed in bronze, a fine maille hauberk, and a sword that would have brought joy to any warrior's heart. Evan caressed the hilt, focused all his strength, and held the weapon up to mirror the light. No doubt the sword possessed a wonderful balance, but it was a dead weight in his hand. Without Martin's timely intervention, he might have dropped it before he could lower it to the table.

"One thing more," Osric added, "I return to you the fief of O'Byrne and all the rights and privileges thereto pertaining."

Yet best of all, beyond any physical gift that Osric might have presented, was the gift of being called by the royal name of the king's line. Evan had been born a MacKeth, but Osric had honored him with the name Murchadha.

Soon thereafter Evan departed, so exhausted he could barely stay awake. As he was carried away, there was one who watched him longer and with keener interest than any other: Anwend Halfdane.

The dim light from sconces cast an uneasy glow against the walls and floor of the hallway. Evan closed his eyes as he was borne along, and let the gentle rhythm lull him to sleep. Yet no sooner had he drifted off than he was jarred awake again.

"Beg pardon, lord," offered one of the servants as he adjusted his grip on the chair.

"Be careful, can't you?" scolded Martin. "You might have dropped him!"

"Mind yer manners, youngster," warned someone who nudged Martin, none too gently, out of the way.

"Stop!" cried Evan.

"Beg pardon, lord."

"Stop I tell you!" Evan insisted. "In there. Take me in there!"

"Ain't nothin' in there, master. Just an empty old chapel."

"I know what's in there. Open the door."

Once inside the shadowed room, a chill of remembrance washed across Evan like an ill breeze. His throat tightened. "Wait outside," he commanded.

The room was indeed a chapel, though it hadn't always been. In place of the bed was a carved wooden altar. A stone basin in an iron stand had replaced the wardrobe that once stood against the wall. But more than the memory of furniture, of what had covered the walls and stood in the corners, the recollection of what had transpired there filled Evan with a flood of emotion.

There beside the window where the table once stood, Osric had taught him to play chess. On the balcony, Ivrian had instructed him in courtly protocol before his first royal banquet. And there on the floor, Maeve MacKeth, his mother, had breathed her last.

The room was filled with spirits of the past, joy and sorrow, calm and chaos, but a strange peace surrounded everything now. It rested upon Evan's heart like a friendly embrace.

"Did you hear, mother?" Evan whispered. "I've been given O'Byrne. Everything is all right now, but I suppose you know that, don't you? But I must know: Are you alright?"

"She is with God," Julian said solemnly.

"How do you know?" Evan asked, brushing away tears.

"I just know."

"I miss her."

"You will see her again one day. Until then, rejoice in her salvation as she rejoices in yours."

Across a small, shadowed room, two men faced each other.

"Do you think you can distance yourself?" demanded one of the other. "You *will* cooperate, if you want to keep your pitiful head on those cowering shoulders."

The second man took a deep, shuddering breath and ran his hands over his face. He was sweating despite the cool evening air. "I have a reputation based on sound business dealings," he complained. "I'm risking everything I have!"

His companion answered with an outburst of thin, horrifying laughter. "And if you refuse? Think of your family, Baldwin Oakshotte--your wife and children, especially your children."

His words were ice, freezing Baldwin's blood. "Leave my children out of this. Haven't I given enough already--the great bronze icon of Moloch that stood before the temple? I paid for that!"

"That was then and this is now," growled the priest with a dismissive wave of his hand. "That bronze statue was melted down when King Osric banished the Priesthood; the temple isn't even there anymore. At any rate, surely you don't believe your success has been due to your own efforts. Do you, dear Baldwin?"

Baldwin trembled. He had placed himself in Claranides' hands long ago, and now those hands were at his throat. But he knew that Claranides was right: everything he had, all that he had attained was tied to the Priesthood. If he could face this last challenge, the reward would be incalculable. At any rate, he had no choice. "Command me," he said.

Claranides smiled without warmth. He hadn't spent so much time and money only to be frustrated by an insignificant merchant. The High Priest was tempted to have him removed, but he wanted to avoid suspicion as long as he could, for Baldwin Oakshotte was the key to this delicate matter; or rather, he sat upon the key. "Show me," he said.

Baldwin led the way through the fine stone house with its rich furnishings and lavish rugs. He had done quite well. He had even roofed his home in great sheets of beaten copper, as much to symbolize his wealth as for any practical reasons. As he passed each icon of his success, he despaired of losing it all.

They descended a narrow stairway to a tiny basement that had been laboriously carved from the rock of the bluff. Though entirely empty, there was a curious design traced out in red paint on one wall. Claranides lay his hand against the stone. "Men will come," he said. "Do their bidding." His eyes bored into Baldwin's soul. "Don't disappoint me, dear Baldwin."

Giomer Lorich was a worried man. As commander of the Legion detachment in the town of Gwenferew, he was responsible for the safety of the four thousand souls who had made their homes within its walls. Fast on the border with Goth, the town was in constant danger from the depredations of savage northern tribesmen who often swarmed down upon homesteads and travelers, pillaging, torturing, murdering.

But Giomer had cut his teeth on battle. As a young legionary he had fought at Fort Cailte where for twenty-three days three thousand men of the Second Glenmaran Border Legion had held off more than twenty five thousand Picts. When the relief column finally arrived, the hungry, battered remnants of the garrison had marched out to swell the ranks of King Yuri's army, and there on the plain they had destroyed the Pictish forces. Giomer himself had slain their Chieftain, Morgatha.

Giomer was less comfortable with the politics of his post. Relations with town officials and merchants were usually strained. Military concerns rarely coincided with those of civilians, while traditional rivalries between the town militia and the Legion fomented constant quarreling that often resulted in wholesale brawls. There was even trouble between the Legion and Duke Morleigh Dunroon, who was ill-disposed toward armed legionaries patrolling his nearby holdings. But at the moment, Giomer's chief worry was for his own men.

Four days ago he had sent forty men to patrol west of the town. There had been unspecific reports coming from that region, mostly from farmers or panicky travelers, and with Duke Dunroon in Durham for Spring Festival the matter had been thrust upon Giomer. It had all seemed rather routine until the patrol had gone missing, and though the missing men had been found, slaughtered on the roadway, of the enemy that had laid them low, there was no sign.

———

As Klabaga had expected, there was a general uproar upon his return to the Clan Home of Ugrik. The returning goblins carried back more than two-dozen dead while numbers of wounded struggled along with the column. But they also brought numerous captured arms--swords, javelins, shields and armor. Great excitement heralded his arrival; she-goblins and children milled close around to discover in what adventure the Red Goblin had been engaged.

But, as Klabaga had also expected, not everyone was glad. Ugrik flew into a horrible rage. "I told yer not to attack the man-things!" he howled. "I'll have yer fool head, is what!"

Many of the goblins thought Klabaga had done a grand thing. They had come together to destroy the man town, to pillage, kill and burn, and now one of their own had struck the first blow. But Ugrik would have none of it.

"What does yer want?" Ugrik demanded of his warlords. "What does yer want in yer hearts?"

"Blood!" snarled one of the Greys after a moment of awkward silence. "We wants blood and plunder!"

The others shouted such riotous assent that it seemed there were hundreds of goblins there instead of the few that had gathered.

When the outburst had subsided, Ugrik said, "Then tell me this: When goblin hunters stalk cave boar and crouch beside a dark pool ta wait fer 'em ta come, does they strike down the first one what comes to drink?"

"Why, ya knows better'n that," snorted someone. "The smell of blood'll keep t'others away. Wait for 'em and when they think it's safe and three or four've come ta drink then up and kill 'em!"

The others grunted in agreement. "That's right!" beamed Ugrik. "That's the wise thing.

Wait fer 'em and take the lot. Ain't nothin' different about hunting human men. Does yer want a dozen skulls fer yer lodge poles or does yer want hundreds, thousands?"

Ugrik went on, "Soon the enemy soldiers will stagger from drink and their women will twine flowers in their hair ta celebrate their great festival, and then we'll strike. Then the streets of the man-city will run gutter full with blood, and then yer'll bring away their women and children ta serve yer desires. Be patient and yer'll have that. Be wise like King Lodrak, and yer'll have it all. Nothin will stand before yer!"

Klabaga knew that Lodrak had conquered half the world only to lose it all again, but he said nothing.

"Only wait a bit and then we'll slit their throats." When the others had gone, Ugrik approached Klabaga. "Do that sort of thing again, and I'll kill yer," hissed the chieftain. "Ya don't go out again, d'ya hear? Yer ta stay put till it's time! Understand?"

Klabaga nodded and went back to his quarters. He wasn't worried about Ugrik or his threats; something else weighed upon him. Somewhere the human boy Evan MacKeth cast his eyes into shadow, seeking for the time and place when he would again come face to face with

Klabaga. Somewhere the pair would find each other, and only one would walk away from that meeting. Perhaps he would find the human boy at Gwenferew, on the meadows of tall grass called Clon Miarth.

Back at the encampment Orglyx informed him that three of the wounded goblins had died. They had been stripped of valuables and cast into a deep crevasse--Grey Goblins didn't bury their dead; they disposed of them. Even old King Lodrak, for all his accomplishments and glory, had been left to rot in his own bed until rats had reduced him to a pile of bones. Red Goblins were different. They sealed their honored dead in elaborate tombs and paid homage to their memories. Greys were filth, but they were a means to an end.

———

After the banquet Evan slept the balance of the evening and the better part of the next day as well. He woke in late afternoon to the voices of Martin and the Watcher.

"Now be gentle, can't you?" encouraged the boy, offering the bird a pear. "You nearly took my fingers last time!" The bird took the pear in its teeth and then snapped the whole thing into its mouth. Martin jerked his hand away to save it from a similar fate.

"I see you've made friends with my bird," Evan said.

"Aye, lord," replied Martin, coming to Evan's side. "We attended while you slept and he grew to seem less fierce. An intelligent bird: I think it understands what I'm saying. Where did you get him?"

The question echoed in Evan memory, returning him to the moment when, as a young boy, he had asked the same thing of Julian Antony Vorenius. "I didn't *get* him. The One True God sent him to me. His name is Julian. He's my Watcher, an angel if you prefer."

Martin pulled at his tunic. "An Angel, good my lord?"

"Yes, an Angel," asserted Evan.

"An Angel," clucked Julian, though not in human speech.

Martin tried to remain calm, but he wished he were back in Faltigern.

"No, no, Martin," assured Evan, "I'm entirely serious. Julian, speak to him."

"I won't," protested the bird. "I speak only to you."

"You've spoken to Aine before."

"Only because you were dying! I don't want to talk to Clumsy Boy." He cocked his head toward Martin, who was gauging the distance to the door.

"For pity's sake, Julian," scolded Evan. "You're scaring him to death! Talk to him!"

"You're the one scaring him, going on about talking birds. Have you gone mad?"

"Cruel bird! Won't you listen to me?"

Julian hissed and acquiesced. "I understand you right enough," he said.

"Great mercy!" cried Martin and collapsed to the floor.

He awoke with the strange bird astride his chest, peering down into his eyes. "Did you truly speak to me?" Martin wondered out loud.

"Against my better judgment," snapped the bird. "I was unaware that public speaking would be required when I took this position."

"Position? What position?"

So Evan told Martin how he had come to meet his extraordinary avian friend, of his place as a Warrior of the Son and the wonders of the One True God. He told him of his premonition that something bad was brewing, and how he hoped to find out what it was before it was too late. "Will you help us?"

"My life, noble lord," said Martin with such conviction that it was impossible to doubt his sincerity.

Soon afterward, however, Evan had cause to regret sharing anything with the boy, for Martin's curiosity spiraled out of control. He began asking questions faster than they could be answered, which was both improper and obnoxious.

"Be quiet, Martin!" ordered Evan at last. "Go fetch me something to eat and come back less enthused!"

Martin scurried off smiling.

"Hello, Biscuit."

Aine stood atop the battlements overlooking the confluence of the rivers Gabhailin and Cuinn as they split against the rocky promontory of the Sceir Naid. Here she pondered the paradox of Evan MacKeth, how he filled her with such anger and desire. She had never felt this way about any man, and even the frustration seemed pleasant, if confusing.

"Hello, Biscuit," said the voice again, "have you no words for me?"

She turned to find Eowulf Fitzwarren, smiling as though amused. She returned the smile. "I'm sorry, Eowulf. I didn't hear you. I was thinking."

"And what ponderous thoughts turn in that pretty little head of yours?"

Aine looked up into Eowulf's piercing eyes. Though she had known him since childhood, she didn't know him well. He was handsome, but there was an elusive hint of something cold about him, something hard. Not unlike Evan. She sighed, "The incomprehensible behavior of men. Can you shed any light on the subject?"

Eowulf laughed. "Not I! But I understand cold steel well enough. My blade is at your service. Is there anyone you'd like me to call to task for--what was it you said--'incomprehensible behavior'?"

She laughed. "Of course not."

"Come now, Biscuit," Eowulf urged. "Who vexes you?"

"No one," she answered quickly.

"It's that MacKeth fellow, isn't it? The King's brother? He broke my nose." Eowulf was still smiling but there was an edge to his voice, a menace in his words.

"Yes, I know. But you were both boys then. That was a long time ago."

"Not so long as I'd forget," mused Eowulf out loud. His broad hand gripped the hilt of his sword with such pressure that his knuckles showed white. But when Aine's eyes glinted with alarm, his demeanor abruptly softened. "It's a pity, really," he said. "When I heard he was back I thought I might put a friendly lump on his head at tournament to set things even. But poor fellow, I don't suppose that will ever be possible now."

Aine's eyes filled with tears. "Do you think I care about that? There's more to a man than physical strength: more than cold steel makes up his heart. But strength and steel are all men seem to value. So play with your toys of war and leave me in peace."

"Come now, Biscuit," Eowulf said gently, "why be angry at me? I've done you no harm."

"Why are you calling me 'Biscuit'?"

"It's the name I chose for you, my pretty miss. Just a name."

"I have a name, you know," she huffed.

"Sure and to be certain you do," he said smiling, "and a right pretty name at that, Aine Ceallaigh, but after the likes of that song t'other night, you'll always be my Biscuit."

"Don't call me that."

"And why not? It's friendly. No harm in it. I'm just being friendly." There was a hint of something unfriendly in his smile, as though the upturned mouth was masking something unwholesome.

"Don't call me that. It isn't proper." Aine turned away to look back over the river toward the dim northern horizon. She felt a hand on her shoulder.

"Come now," crooned Eowulf. "Let's don't be cross, you and me."

"If you don't want me cross then leave me alone," she said, trying to move away from him.

But his grip only tightened. "Look, I haven't done anything wrong. Why treat me like I've got the pox or something?"

She tried to shrug off his hand but he pressed close against her, so she turned to face him. The look in his eyes was different now--hard, cold ice had replaced the soft, warm mischief. Fear insinuated itself into the simple annoyance she had felt before.

"Of course you haven't got the pox," she offered, "but I came out here to be alone. That's all. I just want to be alone."

"A little company won't hurt you," Eowulf said in a friendlier tone, but he didn't let go of her.

Aine weighed her next response. She wanted to strike him for daring to lay hands upon her, but she was afraid of provoking whatever was hiding behind his eyes.

Before anything else could transpire, a soldier emerged from a nearby turret and Eowulf stepped back. Aine withdrew without further comment. Obviously, words didn't deter Eowulf Fitzwarren. She could, of course, take this affront to her father, but that might lead to bloodshed and war. She would have to watch out for Eowulf herself.

As Aine departed, Eowulf watched with an intensity that confirmed its dark meaning. "Goodbye, Biscuit," he muttered, but there was no meaning of *goodbye* in the word.

———— —— ——

Never in his life had Martin been so elated at the prospects for his future. His master was a Warrior of the Son, the strange bird some sort of angel, and he himself was now a spy in the royal household. What adventure! He hurried to the kitchens, and upon returning to his master's rooms, was surprised to find one of the visiting Varangians blocking the portal.

"Where do you think you're going, servant boy?" the warrior demanded as Martin tried to get to the door. The fellow towered over the boy like an oak overlooking a shrub.

"My... my master is hungry," Martin offered, "I've brought food."

"Your master?"

"Yes... yes sir. Lord Murchadha... er MacKeth. In there."

The leviathan shoved his hand in the boy's face. "My master is in there too: Lord Halfdane. He is not to be disturbed."

Martin took a stumbling step backward, nearly dropped what he was carrying, and only held on to it by a remarkable display of juggling.

The big man laughed. "Are you a scullery boy or a jester?"

"Neither, sir. I am Lord MacKeth's servant. Your pardon, but he must eat."

"He can wait."

Martin trembled. "He will decide, not you."

The Varangian's eyes narrowed. "I've already decided, jester. Now run along."

The cold wash of fear stole Martin's breath. He took another step backward, looked hopelessly about, and with a shout, charged for the door.

———

Martin had been gone only a short while when Evan received an unexpected guest. "Enter," he responded to the knock at the door.

Anwend Halfdane appeared in the portal. He bowed and smiled, but behind his graceful formality, an uneasy stiffness held sway. "Greetings lord," the Varangian announced. "I am Anwend Halfdane."

"Greetings Lord Halfdane. You are welcome here."

"I bring a gift from my homeland. A token of friendship in remembrance of your birthday." He closed the door as he entered the room, leaving a companion outside.

The Varangian handed Evan a small wooden box carved with scenes of dragons and other, less identifiable creatures. Inside was a small knife with a pattern-welded blade and an ivory grip.

"This is a fine thing!" Evan exclaimed. "Will you sit?"

Anwend flopped unceremoniously into a nearby chair. "It's Varangian steel. There is none finer."

"Varangian steel?" asked Evan. The knife was elegant and light, the patterns in the blade reflecting the afternoon sun. "I've heard tales about Varangian swords."

"Some say they are finer still than the blades of Illyria."

"And yet the Legions of Ascalon are supplied with Illyrian swords."

Anwend shrugged. "It's merely a matter of supply. Varangia hasn't enough foundries to satisfy the needs of Ascalon. Still, when last I was in Pelakapar I noted many Legion Officers carrying swords from Varangia."

Evan's face brightened, then fell. "Pelakapar. Had I made better choices I'd have seen that fabled city by now."

120

"Choices?"

"It doesn't matter," Evan said, but the terrible 'what-ifs' nipped remorselessly at his mind as he contemplated what his life might have been. After a moment he turned back to his visitor. "What brings you so far from home, Anwend Halfdane?"

Anwend hesitated. "The tournament," he said at last. "It is well known."

"Indeed? I should have thought it insignificant in the wide world. Surely you have attended grander spectacles?"

"Every place brings its own reward. No doubt Glenmara will provide one in the end."

"It is my great hope."

"Then with that hope in mind, might I pose a question?"

"A question? Of course, and I will venture to provide an answer."

Anwend gave a hollow smile. "How did you come by your wounds?"

Evan's stomach surged at the unpleasant remembrance. "Surely you've heard by now. Everyone in the palace knows."

"I would fain hear it from you."

"It isn't a pleasant memory."

"Such memories never are. But won't you describe what you felt?"

Evan pulled his injured arm onto his chest as if to protect it. "What I felt? Surely you've been wounded before? There's no mystery."

"I know the sting of steel against my flesh. But I speak of other things."

"What do you mean?"

"You know what I mean. You can still feel the ice and fire in your bones, can't you?" The Varangian rose from the chair, his face twisted in a hideous rictus of terror and loathing. An awful emptiness filled the room, and it seemed that at any moment Anwend would seize Evan and destroy him.

But just then, such a cry and commotion erupted from the hallway that the attention of both men was drawn to that quarter. The door burst open and a tangle of limbs struggled across the threshold.

"What mischief?" Evan called while Julian hissed and whistled in alarm.

"Gervald!" roared Anwend, suddenly himself again. "What are you doing?"

"I told this little rat not to interrupt you!" complained Gervald as he held poor Martin off the ground with one hand collared about his tunic.

"Release him!" Evan commanded. The Watcher took flight and hovered nearby, ready to do as may. Anwend nodded and reluctantly, Gervald released his undersized opponent.

"Thank you for the gift, Lord Halfdane," said Evan. "Now I bid you good day."

Anwend bowed. "Your pardon sire," was all he said, but Evan read heavy disappointment in his eyes.

When the Varangians had gone Martin fell to his knees in shame. "Forgive me, Master," he cried, "but what was I to think with that giant blocking the doorway? He wouldn't let me pass!"

"So you decided to fight your way inside?"

Martin lowered his head. "I shall return to the Herald."

"Nonsense. I simply never expected anyone to exhibit such bravery just to bring me dinner. The fellow was three times your size! Now fetch more food. After that I want you to keep an eye on Anwend Halfdane. He didn't come all this way for the tournament."

CHAPTER VI
Love

Late of an evening in the week before Spring Festival, Father Phillipus Mauritius, a priest of the One True God, arrived from distant Ascalon. He was a tall man, so gaunt that from a distance he appeared ill, though he was made of tough muscle and sinew. His face and head were covered with fine, grey hair that intensified the severe look of his eyes, but he was also a jovial man who often laughed.

Dressed in coarse woolen clothing, he arrived on a ragged donkey in the middle of the night. With him came two young novitiates, Brother Flavius and Brother Octavius, who spoke little.

In the following days Phillipus was everywhere as he prepared the Cathedral for the holy ceremony that would christen the beginning of Festival. Aine trailed in his wake asking endless questions, and although Flavius and Octavius were annoyed, Phillipus cheerfully answered every query.

During this time Evan grew so desperate to identify the unseen threat that he confided again in his brother. But Osric proved no help at all. "You'll do yourself a mischief with this pointless worry," Osric advised, but Evan wouldn't be advised.

"They think I'm mad," he muttered. At times he believed it himself. With increasing regularity, dreams haunted what little sleep he did manage-- horrible, sweat-soaked dreams of dark things, death, despair and blood.

Compounding the lack of sleep was the fact that Aine had kept her distance since their quarrel. He was despondent without her, and though he sought strength and solace in the Lord, he remained tormented and miserable.

For his part, Martin was so devoted to his master that one rainy evening when Father Phillipus paid Evan a personal visit, the boy set out on a mission of his own devising.

Father Phillipus had come at the bidding of the King, who hoped the priest could effect a change in his brother. Evan related the story of his salvation and his peculiar position as a Warrior of the Son, and when he spoke of Julian Antony Vorenius, the priest showed great interest. "I knew that man," he said, leaning forward in the chair, "when I was but a novice in Pelakapar. He had a little winged snake or something, didn't he?"

"Yes!" said Evan enthusiastically. "His Watcher, Ezekial. You've seen him?"

"Not in years. And he, too, is a Warrior of the Son? There aren't many of those stout souls left. Yet God must have a special purpose for you since He has given you this gift. But do not trust in your own understanding; seek God's will through fellowship and counsel.

"You speak of dreams and dark visions. To counter them, why not dedicate your life to Iosa? Oh, I know you have done this spiritually, but ceremonially is whereof I speak--a symbolic vigil in the church to affirm your service and renew your spirit in His mercy. Would you undertake such a vigil?"

Evan brightened. "Aye, good priest, I would. Do you think it will help?"

"Can it do aught but help? I have seen this sort of thing produce startling results. Never underestimate the power of Iosa Christus."

The words were comforting, and brought back bittersweet memories of long, star-filled nights with the cold wind blowing down from the ice-crowned peaks of the Iarlaithe Mountains, of a spoiled boy and grizzled warrior discussing the mysteries of God. How he missed those moments! But he had given that up for his own selfish desires, and now Julian Antony Vorenius was gone.

"Trust and obedience," Phillipus encouraged, "These are the ingredients of faith. You have faced a great evil and triumphed by Iosa's Grace, but now there are dark forces working to steal you from His presence. Resist them! Lean upon the word of the Lord and offer yourself as a sacrifice."

"I will, Father," Evan declared.

Phillipus smiled, the dark lights in his eyes dancing like shadows around a fire. "Then come to the church on Festival eve and keep vigil before the altar till dawn. Pray and fast and align your life to His will. I will send Flavius to fetch you. But do not speak of it lest someone try to dissuade you. Deus Vult, my son."

"Deus Vult!" cried Evan.

Phillipus blessed the boy and departed.

"A priest at last," Evan sighed.

"I don't like him," muttered Julian from the window ledge.

"What?"

"I don't like him," repeated the Watcher more forcefully. "There's something odd about him."

"Something odd about *him*?" Evan laughed, "A talking bird thinks the priest is odd?"

Julian ruffled his feathers. "He's just odd."

"What are you talking about? You heard what he said, didn't you? Shouldn't I trust God?"

"I trust God," snapped the bird. "But I don't trust the priest!"

"You're an awful bird," moaned Evan, covering his eyes with his hand.

"Don't like him," mumbled Julian and then fell silent.

———

Martin sought Aine. It was rash by his own standards of caution and knowledge of place amongst nobility, but he was willing to risk anything for his master—including the wrath of the beautiful and dangerous Aine Ceallaigh. Yet when he arrived at her chamber door he paused, contemplating the terrible tortures that would surely befall him were he caught anywhere near her rooms. Still he had to see her, and finding no guards at the door, he ventured to knock.

Aine appeared in the doorway, her hair cascading in glorious folds all about her. It shone like sheets of beaten gold in the dim candlelight and Martin was certain it was improper to see so much hair unbound. He lowered his head.

"Martin? What are you doing here?"

Before his resolve disappeared entirely, Martin took a deep breath and spoke: "I know I rise far above my station, Lady, but I come on behalf of my master who does not know I am come."

"You assume to speak for Lord MacKeth when he knows nothing about it? You do rise high," she said coldly.

"Yes, my Lady, I rise for the sake of my master, who loves you."

Aine's cheeks flushed scarlet and her eyes flashed. "How dare you speak of such things when your master hasn't seen fit to mention them himself? Am I often the topic of conversation, as though I were some common street girl one discusses with servants?" She didn't want it to be like this between Evan and her--secret messengers whispering the longing that neither of them had the courage to speak. Not that any of that was Martin's fault.

"I beg you," Martin said in a tone suggesting anything but begging, "go to him. He waxes wroth..."

"Of course he waxes wroth--at everyone and everything. Before I go near him he must apologize to Brian!"

"He has long since apologized to Lord Beollan, my Lady," countered Martin. He related the event.

Aine's expression began to waiver. The corners of her tightly pursed lips quivered and the hard veneer of her eyes seemed to melt, leaving her looking sad and small. "I will go to him." She kissed Martin on the cheek and disappeared into her room.

Martin walked away with an odd smile on his face, but he couldn't dwell long in the blinding euphoria of that unexpected kiss. It was time to find out what Anwend Halfdane was doing.

———————

Father Phillipus walked toward the Cathedral where he and his students were quartered. Their rooms were small but comfortable, lavish by comparison to what he had enjoyed in his previous post. He was glad to be in Durham at last, glad that he would finally be able to further the faith in Glenmara. And there was much to do. Now there was the king's brother to consider. He was hurrying across the courtyard when a figure loomed up from the shadow, blocking his way.

"Good day to you, Priest," grumbled the figure, pulling back the hood of a heavy cloak. "I am Anwend Halfdane." He bowed.

"Ah, yes," said Phillipus. "The Varangian. I greet you, sir, but will you not come out of this rain?"

Anwend ignored the suggestion. "You're from Ascalon aren't you? From Pelakapar? I've walked the streets of that city many times. We took ship there from Gokstad and then came overland to this fair country. Had the fates been kinder we might have passed each other on the road. Kept company, each the other."

There was an odd inflection in his voice, a certain strained quality about his eyes that made Father Phillipus nervous. "Yes, a pity we didn't meet sooner," he said as he tried to move past.

Anwend grabbed his arm. "Ever been to Glenmara before?"

Phillipus pulled away. "No, but the church has corresponded with King Osric for several years."

"Xulanct is a strange, dangerous place, isn't it?" Anwend commented, "Those people don't like foreigners at all. They tried to crucify one of my men just for speaking Varangian. Wanted to nail him to the city gates along with some other unfortunates they had seized. Can you countenance it? We had to fight our way out. I hope our little escapade didn't cause your party any inconvenience as you passed through that inhospitable place."

By now the priest was soaked through and was convinced the Varangian was drunk. "No, there were no problems, thank you. It's been ever so pleasant talking with you, but I must take my leave. Good night."

Anwend stepped aside. "Oh, one more thing," he said as Phillipus moved past, "What do you know about... Shadow Things?"

Phillipus turned. "What?"

"Shadow Things--creatures that hunt for flesh and thirst for blood. Things that leave their mark upon your soul even if you survive their loathsome touch. Darkness, fire, lingering eternal death."

"Demons? Do you mean--"

"Aye," said Anwend, his eyes kindled with terrible lights. "Demons. Do you know of them? Have you seen them? What can you tell me about them?"

Phillipus took a step back. "I know little of such things," he answered as though he were afraid, "Perhaps we may speak of this again. Good day to you, sir!"

He was gone before Anwend could say anything else or move to stop him, but it didn't matter. The Varangian shuddered from the chill of the rain as he pulled the cloak closer about him. It was folly to be here. But had he stayed in Varangia he would have gone mad by now. Perhaps he was mad already.

Anwend walked away from the church without bothering to take shelter from the steady drizzle. The rain was as cold and uncomfortable as his remembrance. His spirit had been full of shadow since Brigida's death, although *death* was too calm, too clean a word to describe her passing. He groaned, pounding his hands against his head to clear the picture of her softness so brutally torn, but it was an indelible image. A creature of midnight terror had butchered her, and Anwend, mighty warrior that he was, had been unable to prevent it.

He had battled many men, blooded his sword hundreds of times, but neither his strength nor skill had sufficed to defeat the horror that had taken Brigida from him. Sometimes he blamed her for all his misery, though he knew it unfair, but had it not been for her faith in the One True God none of this would have happened. One True God? What did the Varangian Gods, Odin, Thor, and Freya, think about that ridiculous idea? But something stirred in his heart when he thought of Brigida's fierce devotion to the God who had caused her death.

Though nothing in the hierarchy of Iosa's tiny church in Miklagard, Brigida's quiet strength had been its heart. On that terrible, forlorn night the creature had chosen her, and before Anwend could do anything, it had struck her down. Anwend himself had been desperately wounded as he fought over her body, and the chill of that evil touch lingered still.

It was that clinging darkness that had brought him so far from his home to this miserable night. He had come to find Sigrid, Brigida's childhood friend who had wed Robert Fitzwarren from Glenmara, but the answers he was seeking were buried in her silent grave. Yet there had been other developments.

In Evan he recognized the same darkness that haunted his own spirit. If he could tap into that experience, he might better understand his own. At least it was a hope, something positive out of all this wasted wandering.

And then there was the priest. The darkness hovered around him too; Anwend's touch had confirmed it. And the priest was lying about something.

Father Phillipus was not the priest from Ascalon. For in the country of Xulanct, in the shadowed city of Nezadsahr, Anwend had witnessed the true priest of the One True God, the priest he himself had met in Pelakapar, nailed to the city gates with his two followers. The man here in Durham was an impostor--an impostor who knew about Shadow Things.

"You're soaking wet," observed Octavius as Father Phillipus hurried into the empty church.

The priest brushed past and disappeared into the adjoining room. His subordinates followed. "What's wrong, master?" inquired Flavius.

"I just spent several minutes talking to an idiot in the rain. Fool of a Varangian asking questions."

"What sort of questions?" asked Octavius.

"Don't worry about him. I told you, the man's a drunken idiot. The king's brother is a different matter."

"The wounded boy?"

"The same." Phillipus related the story of their meeting.

"A Warrior of the Son here?" howled Octavius. "What does he know?"

"Nothing. But he tells tales of Julian Antony Vorenius. You remember him, don't you?"

Octavius stammered, "Julian Antony Vorenius? Is he here?"

"No. And even if he was, we'd deal with him."

"I knew one of the priests the Temple sent to 'deal' with him a few years ago. They buried him with his six companions."

Phillipus cursed. "Shut up! It doesn't matter. Vorenius is long gone. You needn't worry about him."

"But if Lord MacKeth is a Warrior of the Son... they have powers," complained Octavius.

"He's a cripple! Anyway, I've convinced him to hold vigil in the church on Festival Eve. Then we'll have them both: the king and the Warrior of the Son. That will be your job, Flavius. Get the crippled boy here and kill him. You can kill an invalid, can't you?"

Flavius grinned. "Rather like killing an infant, I should think."

"Precisely. There's nothing to worry about. How is the work progressing?"

"The final wall will be breached tomorrow night, leaving only the floor stones in the back room. Everything is ready in town. But a Warrior of the Son..."

Phillipus laughed. "Be brave, you whimpering thing. The palace will be ours before anyone knows it, and with Robert Fitzwarren on the throne we'll crush the followers of Iosa Christus just as we've planned all along."

———

As Aine hurried through the dim corridors, unseen eyes watched from a shadowed balcony. "Look at that, will you?" whispered Guthrum. "I'll have a taste of that when father sits the throne."

Eowulf coldly replied, "She's not one of your peasant wenches. I'll have that pretty biscuit for myself."

"Why should you have her?" snorted Guthrum, leaning over the railing for a last look.

"Because you haven't the courage or strength to prevent it happening," answered Eowulf with a shrug of casual certainty.

"And what about you, Aelfric?" encouraged Guthrum.

"Pant after Aine Ceallaigh, if you like," answered Aelfric. "In a few days you can pick any woman that suits you."

"Soon," said Guthrum, and the word launched a wide array of thoughts among the three.

Within days their father would seize the throne, and the fortunes of many people would be drastically altered. For Aelfric, *soon* meant that he would be one step closer to his own crown. As the eldest son he was due all the inheritance, which, if he were careful and lucky, would include the kingdom after his father's death. But his impatient mind was whirling about like a mechanical toy.

His father was a hale and healthy man. It might be twenty years or more before Aelfric could realize his full inheritance, and he had no intention of waiting until he was an old man to collect. Even so, his father wasn't king yet, and with the entire plot coordinated and financed by Claranides, Aelfric wondered who would really control Glenmara in the end.

Eowulf had his own visions. As the second son, he was entitled to nothing. Anything he got, whether his father was Duke or King, would be entirely determined by his own cunning. Various ideas crowded his mind, but he had never been able to grasp the finer points the politics of power, and in the end he always resorted to the only thing he was any good at: violence. He had proved himself in countless fights both on and off the tourney field. Indeed, it had been he that had scarred Aelfric's pretty face during an argument some years before.

In a short while Eowulf would find his worth in the frantic press of battle; when it was over, he would take pretty Aine Ceallaigh, willing or not. Maybe he would kill the king's crippled brother too.

Young Guthrum didn't care about any of these things. Being the last in line, there had never been any point in hoping for an inheritance, so he had grown content with the benefits his lineage provided. With his father on the throne, things were bound to get better. Too bad Eowulf wanted Aine though; Guthrum would have liked that bit of fluff for himself.

Leaning out over the railing to catch a last glimpse of Aine, Guthrum lost his balance, and with a slight nudge from Eowulf, nearly went over the edge. He was only saved when Aelfric seized his belt. Guthrum was no sooner on his feet again than Aelfric bloodied his nose, and Eowulf's amusement vanished as his older brother collared him.

"Kill yourselves off for all I care," Aelfric hissed, "but not before we've completed our business." Eowulf glared back but dared do nothing more.

With a snarl Aelfric disappeared into the shadowed palace. Guthrum soon followed, but Eowulf remained for a long time, soothing his injured pride with thoughts of the terrible vengeance he would one day visit upon his brother.

———

Martin reported the strange meeting he had witnessed between Anwend Halfdane and Father Phillipus. "A strange fellow, on my word," Evan mused. Watch him; we don't want him harming our priest."

Julian mumbled something unintelligible and ruffled his feathers.

Martin was changing his wet clothes, Julian was sulking in the window watching the rain and

Evan was considering their odd Varangian visitor when someone knocked at the chamber door. Aine peered in and Evan was suddenly concerned with nothing else.

"Come," he said.

There was a hesitation in her step as she came into the room, an uncertainty written across her face, and it appeared she might burst into tears at any moment. "I know you apologized to Brian," she said at last. "Why didn't you say something?" She rushed to his side, took his hand and placed her own against his cheek.

The simple touch filled Evan with a desire that welled up like an overpowering flood. "I love you," he blurted.

Aine felt the blood surge across her face. "What?"

"I love you, Aine Ceallaigh," he repeated. "More than sunlight, more than the breath that sustains me. I value my love above kingdoms or riches or the restoration of my health or the promise of one more day. And should you not love me, should you find me unfit, I will love you still and will find no fault in you. I love thee, Aine Ceallaigh, and it's ever I shall."

Her eyes grew wide and filled with tears as she shuddered from the emotion that rushed through her. "If you knew how I've longed to hear that, you'd not have waited," she scolded, but then she was embracing him, kissing him.

It seemed to Evan that his entire existence was centered in that one extraordinary, exhilarating kiss. Never before had any physical event encompassed so much feeling.

For her part, Aine was unprepared for the depth of her own emotion, which seemed to grow deeper the longer they clung to one other. She grasped his auburn locks and pulled him closer, wanting to forever bury herself in this trembling instant. She had never been happier, had never felt more alive.

And when at last this token of their love ended, Aine sighed and wept while Evan held her. "My darlin' Aine," he whispered.

Martin smiled and quietly left the room. He was glad that he had been party to bringing them together, though he felt a certain melancholy knowing that someone like Aine Ceallaigh could never belong to someone like him.

After a moment Aine kissed Evan again, producing a pleasant reassurance that the first hadn't been a dream or an un-reproducible phenomenon.

"Even MacKeth," she laughed, "have you kissed many girls?"

"Of course not. Just you, my sweet."

"And yet how is it possible that our first kiss should be so perfect, so professional?"

"Professional?" puzzled Evan. "Not a word I'd use to describe a kiss, but even so, I wouldn't ask you how many boys you've kissed. Is it many?"

"Never so," she said and kissed him once more.

"Besides," said Evan, when he could, "we've had some practice, you and I. I kissed you first some months past."

"That doesn't count. You took that one by force. Trade this for it," she countered and their lips met again.

She was playful now, her smile so radiant that it would have inspired a condemned man. She looked into Evan's eyes, stroked his hair and traced her fingers across his face. The young man was staggered that so much feeling could course through him yet leave him alive.

"Aine," he whispered. The name filled his senses with unfamiliar excitement.

"Say it once more," she breathed.

"Aine," repeated Evan.

"Not that, silly. The other."

"I love thee, Aine Ceallaigh, and it's ever I shall."

"And I love thee, proud Evan MacKeth. But I've loved you longer, ever since you were a prisoner in my father's castle. Thus I love you more!"

"It isn't possible." protested Evan. "If you loved me more, your frail little body would simply collapse!"

Aine laughed, the sound brightening the otherwise dim room. "My frail little body, is it? Oh Evan, were I not a lady, I'd box your ears. But I shall forgo that pleasure for now. I will return tomorrow and perhaps do it then."

"Must you go?"

"Don't expect I'll kiss you again, brazen boy. If you truly love me you'll ask my father's permission to court me. I expect action, not just pretty words."

"I'll speak to your father," Evan assured her, "but if I shouldn't recover..."

"Should you never rise again from your bed, yet will I love you, Evan MacKeth," she said. Smiling and touching his cheek once more, she left him there, stunned, exhausted, but ridiculously happy.

———

Martin wandered the palace. His happiness at having managed something worthwhile was surpassed only by the fact that he had helped his master and Lady Aine Ceallaigh. It seemed too good to be true.

Smiling in a foolish, glassy-eyed manner that would have caused the casual observer to think him drunk, he wandered the dark corridors. Occasionally he passed soldiers of the King's household guard as they stood their posts, but he scarcely noticed them, and they paid him little heed. He walked on, past the great hall, its dark interior yawning like the maw of some terrible sleeping beast, past the winding stair that led to the tower of Torgal the Terrible, past the place where he had first laid eyes on Lady Aine Ceallaigh. Finally, he came to a small alcove along the outer wall overlooking the palace yard and the main gate.

This was his favorite place, a tiny, unused chamber of stone with a single window, no more than an arrow slit really, but it gave a pleasant view of the grounds below. He came here to think and be alone and for the first time since leaving Faltigern he came with real excitement about his future.

But as Martin looked out over the palace yard through the grey haze of rain and darkness, his blood ran chill at the sight of a lone figure outlined against the battlements. It was Anwend Halfdane.

Since his arrival in Durham, Anwend had often been up on the wall. He had a great interest in fortifications, carefully studying any he came across. In Miklagard and Gokstad he had supervised the building of massive stone ramparts and towers to protect the harbors and landward approaches of those cities. He had even been hired to secure the properties of numerous wealthy Varangian families. A master of the architecture of war, he constantly studied how others had solved the problems associated with that science.

In Durham the builders of the fortress had been blessed with a number of remarkable natural features that they had fully exploited. At the confluence of the Gabhailin and the Cuinn, the land rose in a sheer spine of rock a hundred feet up from the water. There was no reliable place to land boats along the river's edge of the fortress except for one small dock directly beneath the shadow of a massive square tower. This dock led to a guardhouse and a series of protected passages that connected to the fortress.

Buttressed walls of heavy stone supplemented the natural barrier of the cliffs along the river's edge. It might have been possible to scale those cliffs and walls, but a young girl with a wooden spoon could have successfully defeated such a suicidal attack. Only on the landward side did the terrain present an even slope that rolled gradually down to the town and finally to the meadows where the fair grounds had been constructed.

In this quarter, walls and towers protected the approach, but here also the architects had performed their most ambitious task. Not content with merely interrupting the hillside with manmade obstructions, they had undertaken a massive work to produce a dry moat that ran from river to river across the promontory. This facing of solid rock stood twelve feet high and served as the foundation for the citadel fortifications bordering the inner town.

Anwend's practiced eyes traced the battlements through the dim darkness of night and rain, back to the fortress gates. Here was the weak point of the defenses.

Gates were the weak points of any fortification, which was why architects and builders took such careful steps to secure them. But here the gates were inadequate and poorly built. It was apparent that the original gates, as well as a portion of the wall on either side, had once been destroyed and replaced with a temporary structure that had never been improved. The walls that should have been twenty feet thick were barely ten, and the stones utilized in the repair were too small to adequately support the mechanisms of the drawbridge; for this reason, the apparatus that spanned the gap between the bluff and the earthen ramp leading into the town was permanently lowered. Anwend believed that any attempt to raise it would result in the collapse of at least one of the towers and perhaps part of the wall, as well. "What a foolish thing," mused Anwend with a sad smile, "to have such a mighty place and lose it to a single stone from a well-sighted ballista."

He shook his head as he looked out over the town at the slate roofs and thatched roofs and even a singular copper roof that shone dully through the mist, rain and chimney smoke. It staggered the imagination to consider how much that copper roof must have cost. Most of the nobility he knew didn't have that kind of wealth, yet here was a town dweller, not even gentry, in all probability just a merchant or moneychanger, who had exhibited his success by building this house with its remarkable roof.

Embellished with flourishes of dark wood and carved marble, the house stood not fifty feet from the rise of the Sceir Naid. It was as popular as it was beautiful, as evidenced by the constant coming and going of people through its doors. Whatever enterprise was being conducted within, business was quite brisk, even at such a late hour, and even in the rain.

"Rain," Anwend said, lifting his face toward the pouring black sky. "And a fool standing in it."

He took one more look at the house with the copper roof, and then turning, made his way back to his rooms and another sleepless night filled with nightmare and sorrow.

CHAPTER VII
The Altar and the Gate

Summoning every bit of concentration and strength he could muster, Evan walked to the door. His courage was strained to its utmost too. The bravery he had shown when he stepped into the mountain to face the Glamorth seemed nothing compared to this act of will. He leaned on Martin for support, took a deep breath, and knocked on the heavy wooden door with his good hand.

Brendan Ceallaigh appeared and bowed. Protocol might have demanded civility, but his expression revealed only distaste.

As he stepped inside, Evan's failing strength was renewed by the vision that greeted him. On a stool, as straight and still as had she been carved of stone, sat Aine. Dressed in a pale blue gown trimmed in dark blue and white, her hands were folded on her lap, and the only things that indicated she wasn't a statue were the lights dancing in her eyes and her measured breathing.

Indeed, Aine had to keep reminding herself to breathe. Since Evan had requested a meeting with her father, Aine had been one great bundle of nerves. The man she loved was coming to ask her father for permission to court her in accordance with time honored tradition, and any number of things could go wrong. What if her father withheld his blessing? What would she do then? What would Evan do? Mightn't the king's brother overrule the wishes of Brendan Ceallaigh? How would her father respond to such an insult? As she shuddered from the awful possibilities that loomed around her like angry clouds, she had to remind herself to breathe again before she fainted dead away.

Evan tried to summon enough moisture in his mouth to swallow, alternating between elation from Aine's presence and terror at the sight of the scowling baron. Martin kept his face down, not looking at anyone or anything. Aine took another breath.

"Thank you for this meeting," Evan managed to say. "I have come to ask blessing to court your daughter. I am very fond of her."

"Fond?" asked Brendan with an unpleasant smile, "Are you telling me you want to wed the girl or is it something less? Speak plainly lord."

Marriage? It wasn't that Evan didn't want to marry sweet Aine, but the courtship came before any talk of marriage. "I ask your blessing in honor," Evan forced out, not knowing what else to say.

"And if I say no?" posed Brendan. He had no intention of handing his daughter over to the first arrogant upstart that asked. He'd go to war if necessary! His eyes seethed defiance.

"If you say no then I'll beg you allow me to prove myself worthy. But if you find no worth in me then I'll withdraw my request. I'll not force Aine to choose between us, and I'll not dishonor your house."

Brendan's voice caught in his throat, his anger made impotent by the strength of the boy's words. He glanced at his beloved daughter, his youngest, the last of his line. She was staring straight ahead as though she were somewhere else, her bright, clear eyes dull and vacant.

He sighed and ran a hand through his beard. He didn't like Evan, but that dislike was based on changed circumstance. Evan's words made it plain that this wasn't the same bitter youth Brendan had captured some months before. And now his Aine was in love with this... this boy. He sighed again and the stern, angry veneer fell away.

"What do you say?" he asked Aine.

Her eyes sparked with sudden hope. "I accept most willingly."

"Most willingly indeed!" snorted Brendan. He turned back to Evan. The boy was pale, weak, and frightened, causing Brendan's heart to soften even more. "You have done my house honor," he said. "I'll consider your request, and give my answer once Festival is over."

Evan bowed politely. "Thank you my lord," he said, but his disappointment was evident.

"Patience," he kept telling himself as he struggled to stay on his feet for just a little longer. He turned to go, stumbled and grasped Martin's shoulder for support.

"Wait!" Aine cried as Evan reached the door. She gathered up a strip of green cloth, curtseyed to her father and said, "With your permission."

Brendan threw up his hands, grumbled, but said nothing.

Evan's breath caught in his throat, and his stomach filled with swarms of somersaulting butterflies as Aine approached. She placed the length of embroidered silk in Evan's hand. "Will you carry my token?" she whispered.

"M'lady, I cannot uphold this precious name in the lists," he said.

"Never mind that," she replied. "Wear it, and you will honor me."

Soon afterward Martin helped his master back to his room where Evan quickly fell into a deep sleep. Martin watched him for a while, finally turning to Julian who was sitting in the window.

"Do you think he'll ever get better?" Martin asked the bird.

"Only God knows," replied the Watcher, but the boy couldn't understand.

"Why can't you talk so I can understand you?" complained the boy.

"Why can't you listen so you can understand me?" snapped the bird.

The argument in two languages went on for some while.

———

At the same hour that Evan MacKeth received the token from Lady Aine Ceallaigh, a council of war convened in the Legion fortress in Gwenferew. Giomer Lorich had gathered his officers: Tribunes, Ronan and Arden, and Centurions Orri, Einar, Roland, Ulik and Dermott.

The forty dead legionaries belonged to Einar Thangmartsen's century. Einar had found their bodies, brought them back for burial, and now gave his report as though nothing out of the ordinary had happened. He was a Centurion.

"They were all dead," Einar said. "There was no camp, no fires. I think they were trying to reach a field of boulders when their formation came apart. They were scattered all over the roadway. Some had been mutilated.

"I assumed Goths responsible until we found this." He placed a folded square of bloodstained cloth on the table. "One of my men saw a bird trying to get under a rock to have at this."

Inside the wrapping were three long, grey fingers covered with dried blood. Though not yet badly decayed, they gave off an awful stench.

"What is it?" asked Roland, leaning over to get a better look.

"Fingers of a sort," mumbled Ulik.

"But from what?" inquired Giomer. Einar shook his head and shrugged.

"A goblin," whispered Centurion Dermott as though afraid to be heard, but he might as well have yelled the words for the effect it had on everyone.

"What!" demanded Ulik, jumping to his feet, nearly upsetting the table.

"A goblin did you say?" snickered Roland. "More likely just fingers left out in the sun too long."

"What do you know about goblins Centurion Dermott?" demanded Tribune Ronan.

"I've seen one sir," countered Dermott with a deadly look at his peers. "When I was a boy, hunters from my village found a dead goblin in the mountains, and we all saw it. If those aren't goblin fingers then what are they? The sun has turned your brains to raisins, Roland, if you think those came from a human hand!"

Giomer pulled the strange fingers closer for a careful look. "Goblins, eh Dermott?"

Dermott nodded. "It was long ago when I was but a wee thing, but I remember thinking that with long fingers like that goblins must truly snatch children from their cribs just like my mother said."

"Well, there must have been lots of them to have gotten the best of Optio Zall, and since you found no camp, they must have been out in daylight. Not an encouraging thought. Ronan, send a messenger to inform Duke Dunroon. I'll write a letter."

"Duke Dunroon is in Durham for Festival, Domini."

"Then send the messenger to Durham. Dunroon needs to know."

"Shall we send word to Fort Cailte?"

Giomer hesitated. If he sent dispatches to Legion Headquarters and this turned out to be nothing, his career would be ruined. He'd be sent to some obscure garrison, relegated to counting spears and shields and boots. He could hear them laughing now: *Giomer is afraid of things that go bump in the night!* But if there *were* goblins rampaging about the countryside he dared not wait.

"Yes, send a dispatch to Fort Cailte as well," he replied, "messengers to leave within the hour. We'll send a finger with each rider and keep one for ourselves. Before we're done perhaps we'll add a few more to our collection. Get my scribe in here!"

———

The sun was setting. The shimmering rays of dying light painted the rivers with splashes of crimson and gold, reflected on the stained glass of the cathedral windows and danced atop the singular copper roof out in the town.

The town was still so full of people moving here and there, carrying bundles, bales and boxes, that one might have believed it noon and the zenith of the day instead of dusk and its ending. Everywhere, everyone made last minute preparations for the morning when Festival would begin.

The evening wore on and deepened. Eager for anything that might take his mind off of the yet unanswered question he had posed to Aine's father, Evan lit three candles in the chapel, one each for the Father, the Son, and the Holy Spirit. There in the dim light of the tapers, girded in maille, his helm and sword arrayed at the foot of the altar, he pledged his life to God.

Osric tried to sleep. He was glad that tomorrow all the careful preparations would finally fall into place one way or another and Festival would proceed as it always had--with a life of its own. His mind wandered back to a Festival when half the fair grounds had burned to the ground with a calamitous loss of life and property. Still, one didn't normally associate Festival with disaster.

Anwend stood upon his wall and watched people filing into the house with the copper roof. They went in but didn't come back out. How would he defend this poor excuse for a gate? What was he doing so far from home? Who was this Father Phillipus, and why was he really here? Why was his beloved wife dead? He shuddered as the endless questions crowded his tortured mind and twisted at his sanity. How glad he would be to lose himself in the violent elation of the Grand Tournament where the sweet sound of shattering lances, the cries of men and the scream of horses would lessen his pain if only for a little while.

In the house with the copper roof, Baldwin Oakshotte fretted as his home filled up with hard looking men. They ate his food and drank his wine and some of them eyed his wife until he sent her upstairs with the children. He longed for the sunrise and tried to keep his mind away from thoughts of the gibbet, the stake or the headsman's axe.

Claranides' eyes burned with a fever that frightened even those who knew him well. No one wanted to speculate what was going on in his dark soul so they left him alone and waited for instructions. It would all be over in a few hours.

Aelfric, Eowulf and Guthrum waited impatiently in their rooms while out in the town their father moved his retainers into position. Only a few more hours.

A fog began to roll up from the rivers like a great, grey, billowing beast that crawled steadily across the festival grounds, up into the town and settled at last upon the Sceir Naid. From the little alcove Martin watched the thickening mist mold itself against everything it touched until it looked as though the palace had been built among the clouds far above the solid ground of earth. Even the brightest lights burned pale, and sounds echoed strangely in the insulated air making it difficult to ascertain their source or cause. But

Anwend Halfdane stayed on the wall and Martin watched him, waiting for what he did not know.

The night wore on, deepened and wore on.

The fog crept over the walls of the Sceir Naid, coiling around Anwend like some ethereal serpent sent to drag him down into the abyss. It had been on a night such as this that his beloved bride had been torn from him, from such mist that the Shadow Thing had come. Bitterly, he willed it to come again and destroy him. He would dance a sweet dance with it before he died! But nothing came save the chill air that weighed upon his aching body, and at last he turned back toward the palace. Martin followed.

The night deepened. The Palace slept. Dawn approached.

———

Unlike most men who eagerly lay themselves down after a day of hard toil, Anwend approached such repose with trepidation. He had long been accustomed to the pain of life, having no expectations of the morrow save more despair, more sorrow. Sleep might have been a blessed relief but for the dreams.

Dreams of terror and madness had driven him here. In these twisted visions his wife screamed and pleaded for her life. The surrounding darkness was filled with such fathomless evil that Anwend felt he was drowning in it, and each day found him weaker, closer to collapse, nearer to insanity. Even drink failed to ease his torment.

This night was the worst he had known. Sinister shapes stalked through his mind, clawing at his soul until he found himself screaming and choking on his own tears.

"Peace my Anwend." Brigida's tender voice cut through the despair like a gentle breeze dispersing dark clouds.

"Where are you?" he cried. "My love, where are you?"

"I am here my Anwend, I am with you." Suddenly she appeared before him, and at the sight of her unblemished beauty Anwend wept.

"Don't weep for me," she said with the same, beguiling smile that had captured his heart so very long ago. "I am with Iosa now, beyond grief, beyond even death."

"Come to me," he begged, reaching to hold her, to bury his face in her dark hair and smell the sweetness of her body.

"I cannot, my love," she said. "I am no longer flesh that you might embrace me. But do not grieve for me, Anwend. Rejoice in my salvation; rejoice in the power of the One True God and the strength of His wisdom. Only seek Him, and He will be always with you. This, beyond all things, I wish for you."

Then her face grew stern. "The terror that stalks your spirit is sent to confuse you. Resist it! There is something you must do." She turned as if to go.

"Wait! Stay with me, please, I beg you!"

"I cannot stay my Anwend," she said. "But heed this and mark it well; you must not let them open the gates. Keep them closed, my love, and know that I am always with you." Then, as abruptly as she had appeared, she was gone.

Anwend gave a great heaving cry as he awoke. Stumbling from his bed, screaming out his wife's name, he thrashed about the room, overturning furniture and pulling down tapestries in his grief. At last spent, he collapsed to the floor.

Brigida! He had seen her! But this last glimpse seemed but a curse, a horrible, haunting reminder of his loss. He was left with a single desire: to join his wife whatever the cost. Anwend's shaking hand brought the dagger to his throat. He tensed, anxious to be done with the torment of his life.

Now! Go to her! Now, you cursed fool! But as these words of despair shrieked in his head, another quieter voice somehow overpowered them. The last vestiges of his sanity seized upon the echoes of Brigida's final imperative. *"You must not let them open the gates."*

Blinking, Anwend lowered the dagger. What was he doing? If he died, who would stop them from opening the gate? That's why he was here. That was the whole purpose of his long journey from Varangia—to guard that wretched excuse for a gate, and though he didn't know why or from whom he was to protect it, he would do as Brigida bid him. Blessed, beautiful Brigida!

Anwend armed himself and stole out into the corridor. Heading toward the outer courtyard, he failed to notice Martin following close behind.

———

Lying on the cold marble floor, Evan sought God's Will. As the night passed, his prayers became disjointed, jumping from place to place as he drifted in and out of sleep. Soon he lost all sense of time, finding it difficult to even remember why he was there.

A bewildering array of thoughts twisted through his mind: thoughts of Aine and Julian, Osric and Anwend and the Red Goblin Klabaga, but at length the pain in his arm pulled him back to the dark reality of the chapel.

Evan tried to move, but it was as if he were chained to the floor. Unable to roll over or gather the strength to push himself to his knees, he called out, hoping that someone would hear him, but only the echoes of his own feeble voice returned.

There was nothing else to do but pray. It was nearly dawn.

———————

An urgent pounding on the chamber door disturbed Osric from much needed sleep. He lingered for a moment in the warm comfort of his bed hoping the noise wasn't real, but it continued, and at last its insistent nature forced him to attend. Outside he discovered Eochad and Octavius.

"Well," snarled the King, "what is it?"

"Majesty," whispered Eochad, "your brother has fallen ill."

A terrible fear flooded Osric's heart. Not Evan. Not after all he had already been through. "I will go to him," Osric said and immediately started down the hall.

"He's in the church, lord," said Octavius as though it were an apology, "Father Phillipus is with him."

"Whatever is he doing there?" snapped Osric.

Before Octavius could complete his explanation, Osric broke into a run. "Fetch Torgal!" he commanded his Seneschal.

Instead, Eochad lingered in the deep shadows against the corridor wall, reluctant to leave the safety and anonymity of that darkness. But there was no use hiding now. It had begun.

———————

Osric found his brother lying on the church floor, a lone figure stooping over him, the scene only visible at all due to the dim light cast by three guttering candles on the altar. "Evan!" Osric called out.

The boy stirred. "Osric," he mumbled, "what are you doing here? Never mind, help me sit up."

"What are *you* doing here is a better question," responded Osric, supporting his brother with his own body. He was heavy, a dead weight in armor.

"Holding Vigil," Evan grimaced.

"What were you thinking?" scolded the king as he stroked his brother's sweat dampened hair. He was so full of love for his sibling at that moment, and he so wished that he could heal all his hurts, that tears welled up in his eyes.

"Father Phillipus suggested it," Evan said, drifting. The only thing keeping him awake was the pain.

Osric addressed Phillipus. "I've sent for my physician. You might have killed him."

The priest threw back the hood of his robe to reveal the glowering face of Claranides in the candlelight. "Quite so," the High Priest said. "I've already killed you both."

Before Osric could react he was seized by a dozen pair of strong hands and wrenched violently to his feet. Evan collapsed in a motionless heap to the floor.

"What's this!" roared Osric. "I'll see you on a stake!"

Claranides slapped the king across the face. "You'll simply die. But before that, Moloch will have you. Bring him!"

They bound him and lifted him onto the cold stone slab of the altar. Though Osric fought, yelled and threatened, there were too many to resist.

"What about this one?" asked Phillipus pointing down at Evan.

"Let him watch," Claranides replied.

Despite the fever, despite the pain and exhaustion, when Evan was dragged to the altar his mind was completely clear. The Watcher's words pounded in his head, completing his despair. *"I don't like the priest."*

The evil they had searched for was upon them and they were helpless against it.

Anwend Halfdane slipped through the fog. He could barely see the steps leading to the courtyard, and nothing more than a few feet away, but the gate beckoned from the unseen distance like a silent promise of redemption. This time he wouldn't fail. This time he would have nothing to regret afterward.

But what made him think anyone would even try to open the gate? How foolish he would look standing there armed cap-a-pie while nobody paid him the slightest notion. He'd be laughed out of town!

Anwend shook his head. He was listening to the wrong voices again. Whatever happened, no matter what anyone thought or said about it afterward, no matter if he lived or died, he would follow Brigida's instructions.

He was following the outline of the church wall when a door opened behind him, and as Anwend hid behind a tree the king and the servant of the false-priest Phillipus hurried past. The pair disappeared into the church.

Keeping to the curve of the wall as it intersected the battlements, the Varangian soon reached the pillars supporting the gateway arch. There was no sentry, and Anwend reached the ironbound wooden doors unchallenged. He waited in the shadow.

It was a short wait. Across the courtyard, through the eerie stillness of the morning air came the dim echo of approaching footfalls. Nearer and nearer they drew until a small group of men emerged from the fog. Anwend knew three of them very well.

Aelfric, Eowulf and Guthrum appeared with three of the king's own guard. They were all well armed, and their hands didn't stray far from their weapons. While they paused several yards away, Anwend turned to the gate.

There was no portcullis. Securing the twin doors was a massive wooden beam that hinged down into heavy iron brackets. A collection of pulleys and a length of heavy rope allowed a single man to raise the bar that would otherwise have taken a half dozen to lift. So while there was yet time, Anwend began cutting at the rope. He wasn't halfway through when Aelfric turned toward him.

"Who can tell if it's dawn in this murk?" he complained, looking up at the sky and cursing. "It must be nearly time. It'll be over in the church soon. Let's get this thing opened."

Over in the church? mused Anwend. The king was in the church. He cut fiercely at the rope.

Aelfric and the others approached but pulled up short when they discerned the lone figure in the shadow.

"Who's there?" growled Aelfric, drawing his sword.

"Pray let there be no bloodshed between us," soothed the Varangian, buying a few more seconds before everything erupted in violence. "It is I, Anwend."

Annoyed instead of cautious, Aelfric came closer, expecting to find Anwend drunk as he had seen him so often in the past. Instead he was pushed back with a sword point against his chest.

"Don't come to me with a weapon in your hand unless you wish to be met in kind," warned the Varangian.

"What are you doing here?" Aelfric demanded.

"I might ask you the same question. Where away on such a miserable morning?"

"We've come to open the gates. Stand aside."

"I think not," growled Anwend as the dagger severed the final strands of rope. "The gate stays shut."

"He's cut the rope!" hissed Eowulf, "What're you playing at?"

"Come closer and see," Anwend invited.

"Open the cursed gate!" ordered Aelfric.

They had barely moved at all when the Varangian leapt among them in a blur of whirling steel. The event was so sudden, so brutal, and pressed home with such force that the group scattered before him, and Anwend bounded back to the gate leaving his foes shaken but uninjured.

"Have you gone mad?" Aelfric demanded. "Go or we'll cut you down!"

"Mad or not, approach this gate at your peril. Mark me or pay the price."

There was a fury in his eyes, an edge to his voice, but Aelfric passed it off as drunkenness and came at him again. He wasn't going to let some half-wit fool of a foreigner stand in his way.

Eowulf watched his older brother go forward, heard a sudden scream and then a sword spun away into the fog. Aelfric collapsed to his knees clutching at the bloody stump that had once been his hand.

Anwend kicked Aelfric out of the way and came back on guard, silent, defiant, still as stone.

"Kill him," ordered Eowulf, "before he ruins everything!"

They surged forward in a loose line only to be met in kind as Anwend charged. Before his enemies could press home their attack he had bloodied Guthrum's face with his shield and stabbed one of the guards through the thigh. He whirled and came at them again.

More screams. Guthrum staggered and fell over the crippled soldier while the others ran. Eowulf, thinking Anwend distracted, feinted low, reversed his wrist and struck for the Varangian's throat. But Anwend refused to drop his shield to Eowulf's ruse. The sword glanced from the iron boss, and Anwend followed with his own sweeping blow that might have disemboweled Eowulf but for his maille. As it was chain links bent and snapped as the blow connected.

A lesser swordsman would not have survived what followed, for Anwend's sword rang violently on Eowulf's blade in a flurry of blows that left the young Fitzwarren gasping. Yet just when it seemed the Varangian must surely kill him, Anwend rushed back to the gate.

Those trying to raise the bar abandoned the effort. Guthrum and one of the soldiers fled; the third dropped like a stone from a blow to his helm.

Panic clawed like unseen hands at Eowulf's throat. Half of his party was already down, and the only thing that had saved his life was Lord Halfdane's decision to change targets. This small foreigner was more skilled than any of them— than all of them together. They couldn't get past him, and they couldn't get through him either.

Eowulf ran for the church. There were men there who could help them--Claranides' people who had come up through the narrow tunnel beneath the walls.

He pulled on the church door, found it locked and hammered at the wood with his sword hilt. There was no answer; the silence screamed of disaster. What if they weren't in there? What if they had all been betrayed? He could feel the hangman's noose tightening, the cold certainty of the executioner's axe against the back of his neck.

"Lord Eowulf," came a voice from the shadows of the church wall, "What's wrong?"

Eowulf whirled about, saw Evan MacKeth's servant boy approaching and did his best to kill him. But he was off balance, startled, and his sword whistled through empty air as his intended victim scrambled away into the fog. He was still searching when Flavius called out through a tiny window in the church door. "What do you want?"

Eowulf raced to the door. "We can't open the gate!" he hissed, "That fool of a Varangian cut the rope!"

"What?" stammered Flavius. "You've got to open the gate!"

"Send some men! Send them now!"

Flavius hesitated for a moment but retreated as Eowulf tried to reach through the window. There was the sound of more swordplay at the gate--another scream, shouts from the wall. Eowulf cursed and flailed at the air. The only good thing to come from this so far was Aelfric's misfortune, though the crushing reality of what their failure would bring made his brother's injury seem insignificant by comparison. His renewed pounding on the door was abruptly rewarded as a dozen armed men came spilling out into the courtyard.

Nearby, Martin was pressed into the narrow niche between the pillars supporting the church doorway. He saw the men come out, saw Eowulf lead them toward the gate, and just before Flavius shut the door again he got a look inside the church.

People were clustered around a single figure tied to the altar. Wasn't that his master there too? What were Moloch's priests doing in the church of the One True God? Fear seized him as the door closed with an awful finality. Suddenly Anwend Halfdane didn't seem nearly as sinister as all those armed men in the chapel.

He pulled at the door, but it was locked. Was that really his master in there? Who was on the altar? The harsh sounds of battle echoed from the gate. Martin felt disaster pressing in upon him, upon all of them, the king, his master, Lady Aine...

Maybe he was wrong; maybe none of this was out of the ordinary. The doings of his betters weren't his concern, were they?

The menace was as thick as the fog—but what could he do? He didn't even have a sword! Martin turned toward the palace and the horn slapped against his back. The horn!

He raised the clarion to his lips and blew the call for enemy at the gates. He wasn't certain it was the correct tune, but he sounded it again and again until he staggered from lack of breath. Then soldiers came into the courtyard, and Martin ran toward them.

CHAPTER VIII
Change of Fortune

S upported between two strong men, Evan watched helplessly as Claranides took his place beside the altar. There was a terrible reflection in the priest's eyes as if the light from the candles had filled them with blood.

"I'll kill you," Evan threatened, though he was too weak to stand. "By all that's holy, I'll kill you!"

"Shut him up!" ordered Claranides and Evan found himself back on the floor, held against the hard stone by a foot across his neck.

He was struggling to rise when a frantic pounding began on the church door, and a terrible pain lurched through his body, leaving him gasping, unable even to scream.

"Iosa help me!" he croaked, and to his amazement, from within the deepest part of his spirit came an answer.

"What do you think He's doing, Foolish Boy?"

Julian? Then a white-hot surge of light burst behind his eyes, and he felt nothing more.

After a time he fancied he could hear a horn sounding the same notes over and over. When he opened his eyes, everything in the chapel stood out with remarkable clarity, despite the dim lighting. Armed men huddled by the door. Claranides, Phillipus and several other priests clustered around the altar where Osric still struggled to free himself. A terrible rage overcame Evan as he lay there at the foot of the dais.

"Foolish Boy, you must get up!" insisted Julian.

Evan rose to one knee. The pain that had marked his every waking moment was gone, replaced by an uncommon peace. He could move his left arm.

"The sword Evan! Take up your sword!"

The blade slipped weightlessly into his hand as he stood. His maille seemed of no more consequence than his tunic. An unfamiliar strength pulsed through his body as he stepped onto the dais, calling out a terrible warning. "This is the House of God! In the name of Iosa Christus, I command you flee or none of you shall see the light of another dawn!"

The priests froze at the unexpected sound of that voice, the uncompromising finality of the words. Osric looked at his brother as though he had never seen him before, while the others in the church hesitated as a silent voice urged them to run for their lives.

But words didn't impress the High Priest. "Kill him," he ordered with a disdainful flip of his hand, and the nearest cleric stepped forward to carry out the command.

The unfortunate priest never completed the step, nor did he ever take another. The wounded boy struck with such measure that his attacker was thrown bodily back into his fellows, his scream cut short in the rush of blood from his slashed throat. Evan vaulted up the steps, scattering those that remained. Even Claranides ran.

Evan cut Osric free and pushed him toward an alcove flanked in stone pillars and statuary. No one moved to stop them.

The High Priest admonished his men, "Fools! Bring them back or I'll flay you all alive!"

They moved toward the two brothers with the cautious certainty of success reinforced by their numbers and the threats of their master.

Watching them come Evan said, "They'll not take you," and Osric believed him. Then the enemy was upon them. Though many, they were hindered by the narrow entrance of the alcove and came on bunched into single file. The first carried a spear.

A spear is a difficult weapon to defend against. It can outreach a swordsman, and delivered with enough thrust can easily part even the best maille. But this spearman was neither accomplished nor prudent. Instantly Evan stepped inside his guard, seized the spear shaft and dispatched the startled fellow. Stepping back he reversed the abandoned spear and hurled it into the chest of the next man.

The room erupted in a chaos of screams and curses. The smell of blood overpowered the stale odors of sweat and fear. The attackers hesitated, weighing their disbelief against the evidence before their eyes, and this pause was enough to change the balance of everything.

A hundred things rushed through Evan's mind, but foremost was the memory of lessons learned from Julian Antony Vorenius. *"Exploit weakness the instant you find it. Take the battle to your enemy."*

He obeyed with silent fury. Three men went down in his initial rush while the rest dispersed with blasphemous oaths that were more prayers than anything else.

He pursued, striking them down as they ran for their lives. Blades cut at him, glanced from his armor, drew blood, but he felt neither blows nor pain. Whoever he faced fell to his remarkable swordsmanship or fled in despair of his power.

———————

The gate was secure. The palace soldiers were dead. Aelfric was too badly injured to be a threat, Eowulf was gone, while bloody-nosed Guthrum kept his distance, refusing to come any closer. Anwend laid his hand against the heavy timbers of the gate and felt the rhythm of steady pounding from the other side. "There, there," he whispered, "we're not taking visitors just now. You'll have to come back later." But at that moment, Eowulf returned with more than a dozen men. The Varangian braced for the onslaught and the inevitable result. "Goodbye," he said. "If You can arrange it, Iosa Christus, if You are who Brigida said You are, take me to her."

He had never before prayed to the One True God, and even now it was less a prayer than a question. Before he could further reflect, the enemy was upon him.

There were too many. In the first seconds of the attack he was wounded again and again, and he knew that in order to protect the gate he would have to move away from it, or they would kill him where he stood. He waded into them screaming, the blood of his foes marking his passage.

He lay about with sword and shield, traded blow for bloody blow, but Eowulf's men were struggling to lift the bar, forcing him back into their midst. He couldn't fail Brigida again.

Yet he was one man. Though possessed of a spirit that kept him on his feet despite the mounting score of wounds and attendant loss of blood, there were still too many. They were raising the bar.

Then something else happened on that wild dawn where so many things came together to alter careful schemes and change the lives of countless persons. A horn sounded, and as though heralded by those crystal notes the sun poured over the walls of the fortress, instantly dispersing the fog.

The men dropped the bar. Now the entire palace would be awake and soldiers would come. Seeing their hesitation, Anwend redoubled his effort and managed to clear the gate once more. Some of his attackers ran for the church while others stood as though turned to stone by the trumpet call.

The whole of the Sceir Naid was now stirring, set in motion by Martin's desperate call in the thin light of morning. Soon the sound of combat rang through the halls as the already violent morning spiraled into full-scale carnage.

Out in the palace yard the soldiers called by Martin's horn moved toward the battle at the gate. In a final despairing attempt, Eowulf and his remaining warriors threw themselves upon Anwend, striking him down by sheer weight of numbers. But even then he grappled with them, clutching and pulling as they tried to raise the bar.

It was enough. With the forces of the king upon them, they fled, leaving their ruined plans among the corpses on the bloody cobblestones.

———————

Above the struggle at the gate, above the vaulting roof of the church beneath which Evan MacKeth fought for his life, Julian the Zalathrax flew. He was trying to find a way into the church to help the Foolish Boy, but it wasn't a simple thing. It was difficult even to think, and flying, which was more natural to him than thinking, was equally difficult.

Only moments before he had been wrestling with sleep on a window ledge, struggling against a troubling, unidentifiable feeling that had wedged itself into his spirit. It was of a piece with an overall sense of foreboding, coupled with his dislike of that priest fellow, and none of these feelings had brought any answers to the ill defined questions they raised. He had grown weary of the foreboding, so he laid it at the feet of the One True God and tried to sleep.

Then, just when he began to drift off, his mind was filled with a vision so remarkable, so horrifying, so glorious that he fell right out of the window.

He knew Evan was in the chapel; he had sensed him praying there for the better part of the evening. He could always feel the intense current occasioned by communion with the One True God, but now the prayer was overwhelming in its fervor and startling in its results. And though the scene he now witnessed in the chapel filled him with fear, his heart leapt with joy as the Hand of Almighty God laid hold of Evan.

"Iosa help me!" he heard Evan say.

"What do you think He's doing, Foolish Boy?"

But now as he tried to find a way into the church, as the Foolish Boy fought against great odds, Julian found it terribly complicated to watch the events inside, concentrate on flying and come up with a plan.

It had been the Priests of Moloch all along! Small wonder he hadn't liked that Phillipus character. That odd Varangian fellow was hard pressed at the gate, Martin was still blowing on that awful horn and who were all those men outside the wall?

There was too much to think about. He had to get into the church or it would be back to the forest for him, back to eating bugs and frogs, with those monstrous eagles to watch out for. He circled the church again, eyeing the heavy, lead traced, stained-glass windows, the massive oak doors, even the arrow slits, but everything was closed, locked, covered. In frustration he turned toward the chimney that rose from the back of the chapel, and with a hiss of distaste, dove down into it like an arrow shot from a bow.

Before he realized what had happened he slammed into the iron vent at the bottom, bounced off the grate, across the stone floor and landed in a bruised, soot black confusion of feathers against the wall.

In the next room the priests and soldiers had rallied. Evan's prowess had been so great that for a time it seemed he alone would defeat the enemy, but now, even with Osric's help, the tide was beginning to turn against them.

The High Priest wiped his perspiring hands on his robe. At the door, Octavius reported sounds of fighting at the gate. The horn sounded insistently above the clamor. Scant moments before the control of the kingdom had been in Claranides' hands; now it was slipping from his grasp in a maddening flow of unforeseen events. He cried out to Moloch for a dark avenger to destroy his enemies.

Instantly it seemed his prayer had been answered. A horrendous shriek pierced the chaotic fabric of sound already present, and into the room flew a small black creature spouting fire from a gnashing beak filled with wicked teeth. It shrieked again, then hurtled full into one of the priests, bowling him over in a flash of fire and black smoke.

The priest screamed. When the nemesis took flight again, wailing like a lost soul and dripping with the blood of the unfortunate cleric, those remaining scattered with a chorus of curses.

Now there was no stopping them. They sought the refuge of the tunnel, crowding and clawing and tumbling over one another in their wild efforts to escape from that place of fear and death. Behind them came Julian, biting, clawing, howling and spouting fire while urging Evan and Osric on.

"Come Foolish Boy! Drive this evil from the house of the Lord!"

In truth, both Evan and the king had been so startled by the unexpected appearance and dramatic ferocity of the bird that they stood transfixed for a moment, uncertain it was safe to move. Now they followed in the bird's wake striking down their fleeing enemies.

Yet not everyone gave way to panic. While his followers fought each other to be the first into the tunnel, and while that activity held the attention of the king, his brother and the horrifying bird, Claranides quickly moved to the door that led to the palace yard. Then unseen amidst the abounding chaos, he and a small group of followers left the church to disappear into the palace.

Others sought refuge in the palace too, their plans shattered, their lives forfeit unless they could win free of the trap their schemes had become. Eowulf left Aelfric behind; the idea of his dancing on the gibbet was the only comforting thought he could muster. Everything else was a disaster, a portent of what he could expect for the rest of his short life if he didn't get out of the palace. Guthrum blundered along beside him, terrified, out of breath.

Eochad was their best chance now. It was his job to capture the rest of the nobility in the palace, and to that end he had a sizeable force of palace soldiers under his command. With Osric dead the others would surely submit rather than sacrifice themselves to a lost cause. They might still salvage something.

The halls of the royal house of kings echoed with the sounds of battle. Somewhere a violent struggle was taking place, and Eowulf hurried to find it. Instead he found Claranides and a handful of other conspirators. "What are you doing here?" he hissed.

"I could ask you the same stupid question," retorted the High Priest, "but the answer should be obvious even to you. We've failed."

Eowulf lowered his head. "Couldn't open the gate," he complained. "That stupid Varangian spoiled it all. But with the king dead..." He looked up hopefully, but the expression on Claranides' face chilled his blood.

"The king still lives," said the priest.

"What? How is that possible? You had your hands on him didn't you? You had forty men!"

"I had *thirty* men before you took half of them, and even then you failed! And I hadn't counted on Osric's brother."

The High Priest couldn't fathom what had transpired in the chapel. How had a sick, crippled boy, suddenly become such a powerful warrior? How had Claranides' own appeal produced the startling creature that had completed their ruin? It didn't make sense.

"Osric's brother? He's an invalid!"

"Not anymore," snarled Claranides. "He drove us out of the church."

185

Eowulf staggered. With the king alive their only option was escape. Let Eochad save his own neck if he could.

———————

The battle in the chapel was over. Evan and Osric gasped for breath as they leaned against one another. Scattered about them lay a grisly carpet of wounded, dying and dead. Blood splashed the walls and pooled in great thickening puddles on the floor. Men cried out in agony from horrific wounds while the stench of death hung over everything with the cloying smell of sweetness.

"What happened to you?" marveled Osric.

"I prayed; God answered."

"If God answers all your prayers like that, you'll be a handy fellow to have around!"

Julian hopped up onto the leg of an overturned chair and began preening his feathers. He was covered in blood. They were all covered in blood, but most of it was from their enemies.

"Are you injured?" Evan asked his brother.

The king shook his head. "There wasn't much chance of that. I won't forget this. I won't forget it--ever. Are you hurt?"

"Scratches," Evan shrugged. "What about you, tardy bird?"

"Tardy bird indeed! You should be grateful I cared to fly down that chimney just to rescue you! No I'm not hurt!"

The escape the conspirators had been seeking was a narrow hole broken through the floor of the room behind the main chapel. From its indistinct shadow came the moans of those who had thrown themselves in to evade death by the sword and those who had been pushed in by the press of others behind. A ladder led down into the depths.

"Where do you suppose that goes?" asked Evan, trying to plumb the darkness. Osric shook his head.

They had just pulled up the ladder to deter other uninvited guests when they heard the outer door slam back against the wall. Someone was coming in—a whole crowd of someones. As Osric and Evan hurried back toward the chapel they heard voices.

"Merciful heavens! What happened in the church?"

"Who are these people? That's a priest ain't it?"

"Moloch's man, that. No business in here."

And then a desperate voice that Evan instantly recognized. "Oh my! My master was in here I tell you! He's been murdered! I'm too late!"

Evan stepped into the room. "How you carry on!" he said. "I'm not murdered."

"My lord!" Martin cried, "I thought you dead! You're covered in blood!" Then the lad broke down and had to be put in a chair lest he collapse.

Filled with reverential wonder at Evan's miraculous healing, the soldiers pressed forward to touch him, but the commotion redoubled when the king emerged. They gathered around their liege, telling of the fight at the gate, the treachery of Duke Fitzwarren's sons, and the brave deeds of young Martin.

Osric placed his hands on Martin's slim shoulders. "You bring honor to my house," he said, and the boy thought he would faint from pride.

No one yet knew the depth of the treachery they faced. Guards atop the walls reported a group of men on the outer ramp of the gate. More than a dozen conspirators lay dead around the inner gateway arch while others had been taken prisoner including Aelfric. Nearly sixty hastily gathered members of the king's bodyguard and palace soldiers were awaiting orders, but many were missing.

Evan felt disjointed, apart from his body. Though strength coursed through his limbs like a tide of molten metal, he had never been so conscious of his helplessness. While a wondering Martin looked on, Evan prostrated himself before the altar. "I am your servant, Iosa. Command me."

When he rose Martin took his arm. "What has happened Lord Evan?"

"The power of God has happened."

"How can I know your God, master? For I would serve Him as I serve you."

"I will show you," Evan said, and together they devoted themselves to His service.

Nearby, Julian performed somersaults in the air.

Awakened by the trumpet, Aine went to the window and peered down into the courtyard, but the fog was so thick that only the notes of the horn gave any indication that anything was happening at all. Soon, however, sounds from the corridor drew her attention--shouts, running and the unmistakable violence of battle.

She quickly dressed. What was going on? Festivities weren't due to begin until well after sunrise, and not before High Mass had been celebrated in the church. Notwithstanding that, there shouldn't be swordplay in the palace for any reason.

Aine listened at the door. Where was her father? Her sister? Evan? Her heart sank when she thought of his helplessness. She wanted to be with him, to protect him, for without him her life was cold and empty. She moved into the hallway, armed with bow and arrows.

The cold stone and wood of the corridors distorted the screams, howls and sounds of battle that echoed through the palace. Her fear grew as her mind conjured wild images, and though she grew more cautious as she proceeded, still she stumbled over the body before she saw it.

One of the king's bodyguards lay in an unnatural tangle of limbs at the foot of the stairs to Torgal's tower; another corpse was slumped against the wall. She had seen dead men before, to be sure, but she had always felt safe in the palace. Aine fitted an arrow into her bow and was about to proceed when she heard voices up the stairway. She retreated to the shadows as they approached.

"What's this about?"

"Didn't you hear the horn?"

"Of course I heard the horn, but what does it mean?" Torgal Umliath came down the steps escorted by four armed men.

"We don't know what it means," growled one of the soldiers, "except we're to get you to the Great Hall."

"Why?"

"Uh, well... somebody's sick. Yeah, it's Eochad. He's sick," stammered another of Torgal's escorts. "We'd better hurry."

Torgal hesitated. Six men of the palace guard to escort him? And where were the other two? Then a muffled crash from above drew his attention back to the tower. "What now?" he complained. He started back up the stairs, but one of the soldiers struck him down with the pommel of his sword.

"Are ya mad?" howled one of the others. "We're supposed to get him to Eochad alive. That one'll heal ya. Don't kill him!"

"Well he was goin' back up so I stopped him."

"He wouldn't heal the likes of you anyhow ya idiot. He's for the royals and that's all."

"Is he dead?" asked another, prodding at the body with the point of his sword.

"What's it matter?"

"Eochad won't like it."

"Eochad can rot. He only wants him for the gold."

"The gold?"

"Yeah, the gold. He turns lead into gold in that tower of his."

"Gold from lead?"

"That's right. I know a man what's seen it done."

"Then why kill him? Keep him alive, and we'll all be rich, ain't it?"

"You're a fool Roderick! Once the Fitzwarren's are on the throne they'll forget who helped 'em get there. We won't see any gold out of this unless..."

"Unless what, Drew?" asked Roderick.

Drew pointed up the stairs. "Ya know what Balthus and Cronk are doin' up there?" he posed. "They're looking for the gold. If we turn Torgal over to Eochad who turns 'im over to the Duke, they'll know about any gold that's stashed up there. If it's gone they'll ask us about it, and we'll hang sure. But if he dies, say while escapin', nobody'll know what treasure we've managed to haul away. But Balthus and Cronk won't share if they finds it first!"

They exchanged nervous glances, carefully weighing the possibilities with the risks. Aine watched from the shadows, the implications of their words conjuring disastrous images in her mind. Duke Fitzwarren on the throne?

None of it seemed real. Not the fact that everything she held dear was now at risk, not the fact that these men truly believed that gold could be made from base metal, nor that because of that belief they were about to commit murder. What was brutally clear, however, was that she was the only one who could stop what they were going to do next.

Aine raised her bow and drew the arrow back to her cheek as Torgal began to stir. She had killed birds and wolves and a great Saber-toothed tiger, but the thought of releasing an arrow against a human being was terrifying. Her sight narrowed until that one small spot on the stairs became her entire world as the tableau paused on the edge of irreversible action. Then another crash from the tower prompted one of the guards to raise his sword.

Aine released the bowstring. She heard a sharp grunt, saw her target stagger, scream and fall. The remaining soldiers scurried for cover, cursing and stumbling as they retreated up the stairs.

"Where'd that come from?" hissed Roderick.

"Balthus! Cronk! Get down here ya greedy pigs! They've killed Welwyn!"

Disoriented, Torgal began to crawl up the stairs toward his captors. A hand reached for him but withdrew as another arrow shattered on the steps.

Aine called out, "Master Torgal! Come away from there!"

"It's a girl!" snarled Drew. He took a single step and fell as Aine's arrow drove to the fletching in his chest. Torgal stumbled out into the hall.

"Find my father!" snapped Aine.

"I'll not leave you."

"You must go! These men will kill you!"

But there was no time. With a sudden rush the soldiers were upon them. Aine fired one hasty shot before she was seized and hurled to the floor. A grunting, malodorous figure pinned her down, and a leering face appeared above her. "I'll teach you what for, little miss!"

Aine brought her knee up with all the force she could muster, and the soldier's face went slack and pale. She twisted free and fled down the hallway until the sounds of pursuit dwindled and disappeared. Eventually she found herself in part of the palace she had never seen before.

At some point Aine had passed from the palace of marble and ornate woodwork into an area of crude functionality characterized by massive walls of rough-cut stone, uneven floors and heavy timbered ceilings. She deduced she had passed into the adjoining fortress where the passage led to the river dock. It was a dead end, and there were always soldiers down there. She turned to go back.

She hadn't gone ten paces when she was seized from behind, her arms twisted cruelly behind her back. A hand found purchase in her hair, and she found herself looking into the merciless eyes of Eowulf Fitzwarren.

"Well," he whispered in a throaty snarl, "this day isn't without its rewards after all."

Aine tried to pull away, only to be rewarded with a blow to the stomach that doubled her over and left her fighting for breath. From the floor she saw that Eowulf wasn't alone. Guthrum peered down at her while the High Priest Claranides looked dispassionately at the scene. Phillipus, Octavius and Flavius gathered close by.

"What are you doing?" asked Claranides as though he were bored. "Kill her and be done with it."

Eowulf's eyes blazed. "She's not for killing. I've come away with nothing. I'll have this at least. Just stand in my way and see what happens!"

Claranides didn't respond. He knew this girl. The tiniest part of an idea stirred in his mind, and he smiled and shrugged. "Bring her along if you like, but she'll be of little use if we're captured. It's a long way to the Hinnom Valley."

"Worry about your own hide," snapped Eowulf. "I might as soon salvage something out of this."

"We wouldn't be worrying about 'salvage' if you'd opened the gate," Phillipus offered.

"So it's my fault?" said Eowulf so loudly that anyone nearby might have heard. "What about you? A crippled boy who could barely walk drove the lot of you from the church!"

"And Anwend Halfdane?" the priest sneered. "You ran from one man!"

Eowulf started toward Phillipus, dragging Aine by the hair. There was a great deal of yelling and jostling, threats and curses after that, and although the girl was sensible to her dreadful predicament, still her heart rejoiced. A crippled boy? Surely that had to be Evan. Was it from he that these men were fleeing for their lives?

She knew of the Hinnom Valley. Beyond the far shores of Loch Aiden, rising up the slopes of the Balinora Mountains, the Priests of Moloch had built their refuge. Even the savage Picts shunned the place. While the others shoved and threatened above her, she pulled an arrow from her quiver.

"If you slaughter each other we will none of us get where we're going," mentioned Claranides. "Either we help each other or go our own way. If we stand here fighting they'll take the lot of us."

"We'll settle this later," threatened Eowulf as he pulled Aine to her feet.

The girl responded as she came up, slashing at Eowulf with the arrow, screaming at the top of her lungs, and for an instant she found herself free. But Guthrum seized her from behind, holding her until Aine embedded the arrow in his leg.

With Guthrum's scream ringing in her ears, Aine bolted back down the passageway, but Eowulf intercepted and felled her with a blow to the side of the head. The stunning pain was the last thing poor Aine was aware of for some while.

Eowulf hurled Aine's quiver down the hallway and approached his whimpering, weeping brother from whose leg the arrow still protruded. "What've you let done now?" He grabbed the shaft, and ignoring the shriek rising from Guthrum's throat, pulled it free in a shower of blood.

"Let's go," he said, scooping up Aine with no more effort than had she been a discarded blanket. "Your screams will bring company." They started down the hall.

Guthrum tried to get up but couldn't bear the awful pain. He collapsed, tried to crawl after his disappearing companions and called out for his brother. "Eowulf! Help me! I can't walk! Don't leave me!"

Echoes were his only answer.

———

The king, his brother and the loyal men that had gathered around them came out of the church into the palace courtyard. The sun was well up now, revealing a scene of carnage rivaling that in the chapel.

Extending from the gate all the way to the palace steps, the bodies of the slain and wounded littered the bloody ground. A guard had been placed beneath the archway in the very midst of the slaughter while nearby other warriors gathered in loose formations or stalked quietly among the corpses.

Information came pouring in. Soldiers on the wall reported crowds of armed men gathering in the streets of the upper town. Parts of the fairgrounds were in flames, and people out in the town scurried about as though lost or pursued. Badly wounded, Aelfric Fitzwarren was discovered hiding among the dead. A young officer of the palace garrison reported that only thirty of his command had answered the call to arms.

Osric gave orders, secured the gate towers and had Aelfric brought before him.

"What treason?" the king demanded. "Speak well and your death may be less unpleasant."

Aelfric was mewling, spittle dripping from his pale lips as he looked up at his sovereign. Everything had happened so quickly that he found it hard to believe it wasn't all a horrible dream. But even his wildest nightmares wouldn't have left him here. "My father will pay ransom," he stammered, eyes wide and laced with blood, "My father..."

"Your father?" intoned the king in a voice so full of ice that even those with nothing to fear trembled. "Your father has enough troubles without worrying about you."

"Lord king, I did only as my father bid me. I am but a dutiful son, not a traitor to you."

"And that's your pitiful excuse for such boundless treachery," roared Anwend Halfdane, pushing his way through the crowd, "because daddy said so?"

The Varangian was a remarkable sight. His armor was torn, his tunic slashed and blood soaked. Little rivers of blood ran down his face, dripped off his chin and spattered his boots with crimson drops. One eye was already swollen shut, distorting his face until he looked more like some grotesque gargoyle leering down upon his prey than a man.

"And what were your father's retainers going to do once inside?" Anwend continued. He grabbed the injured youth by the hair, "A tea party? An early morning game of nine-pins?"

Osric was bemused. It was highly improper to interrupt a king, and he knew he ought to put Anwend in his place. Others looked on aghast as

Samuel Schiller

though expecting the sky to fall from the breach of etiquette. But this was the man who had stood against Aelfric's treason, and had stopped it with his own good blood.

"Mercy great king," shuddered Aelfric, cringing at the Varangian's overpowering presence.

Anwend made to strike Aelfric but Osric interrupted. "Peace, Anwend Halfdane," he said. At those words Anwend's whole demeanor changed, and it seemed to those present that he shrank in size if it were possible.

"Peace my Anwend." It wasn't the king's voice he heard. The words of his beloved wife echoed through his heart, and for the first time in as long as he could remember he felt glad to be alive. "Your pardon majesty," he said with a stiff bow. "This is your house, not mine."

"Never so, Lord Halfdane," said Osric taking Anwend's hand. "This day you have forever earned a place in my house. Why did you do it?"

The authority and power of others had never impressed Anwend, nor did he normally feel out of place in any situation, but somehow he felt small and insignificant now. None of these events had been chance. He told the king his story, and when he had finished, Osric nodded as if it all made perfect sense.

"The Hand of God has moved," he said, "and so must we."

They dragged Aelfric into the church with the other wounded prisoners, set a strong group to secure the walls and the rest followed the king into the palace.

———————

As he hurried toward his chambers for fear that treachery had reached his wife too, Osric's anger rose like an overwhelming tide. Yet in the midst of fear and anger blossomed hope. Miracles abounded. Evan was healed! A stranger had protected the gate, and at least part of the plot had been, if not crushed, discouraged. As for the rest of it, those enemies remaining, those known to him and those yet to be revealed, he would destroy them all, hunt them one by one until no vestige of the treason remained. He would march on Moloch's Temple beyond Loch Aiden and pull that foul abomination down stone by bloody stone. But first he had to win the day.

At his own chambers he found a knot of men standing guard, among them Brendan Ceallaigh and Brian Beollan. Bodies lay heaped near the door, throughout the antechamber and the long connecting corridor.

A great cheer erupted at the sight of the king, and warriors clashed swords against shields. Osric learned of the fight before the door, how traitors had come for the Queen and how these few had set them to route.

"Who dares?" demanded Osric. "Who would lay hands upon my bride?"

Brendan spat upon the floor. "Eochad," he answered.

Inside, Osric found Ivrian, who leapt into his arms, heedless that he was soaked with blood.

"I feared you dead," she whispered, shuddering. "I feared you dead."

"The Lord God of Hosts was with me," said Osric with a conviction that seemed to dispel the oppressive air surrounding them. "He is with us now, and if He is with us, who can stand against us?"

——— —— ——

Seeing Brendan Ceallaigh, Evan thought of Aine. Where was she? Was she safe? He approached the Baron.

Brendan gaped at the young man. He insisted on hearing Evan's remarkable story before he would listen to anything else, and though the youth abridged the events that had taken place in the church, everyone present was awed by his tale. Even little Martin, caught up in the moment, forgot his proper place and launched into a spirited description of the carnage he had seen. Others related the bravery of Anwend Halfdane. A fire began to kindle in the hearts of those gathered, fueled by the certain knowledge that God's Grace had touched them all.

"Lord Brendan," Evan managed at last, "where is Aine?"

"In her room I should think," he said as if it were a foolish question, but before he could say more the king reappeared.

They gathered around him and waited for his command. He said warmly, "I will not forget that in this dark hour you stood beside me and shed your blood. I will purge this treason with fire and sword. I will bring despair and death to the minions of Moloch and I will throw down their temple!"

His eyes shone with terrible lights as he spoke. "I will pay blood for blood. Death to any who stand in my way now!"

There was silence for a moment, a breathless pause where no one moved or spoke, feeling that to do so would be sacrilege.

"Who follows me?" whispered the king but it might as well have been a roar.

They answered with a roar of their own, and amidst the clash of crossed swords, pledged their fealty to Osric Murchadha, his lineage and his God.

———————

Flying over the town, Julian was disturbed by what he saw. He had left Evan to find out what was going on, and now knowing, he didn't like it in the least.

Scores of armed men rampaged through the town, breaking into shops, carrying away bundles of purloined valuables, setting fires and randomly destroying anything that appeared breakable. Some dragged people into the street and murdered them in full view of the soldiers manning the walls of the Sceir Naid.

Fighting had erupted nearly everywhere. Soldiers loyal to the king barricaded themselves in guardhouses and other strong buildings, but there was little these fragmented groups could do. Quickly the control of the town passed into the hands of Robert Fitzwarren, and although the pillaging, burning and rapine continued, a certain brutal order established itself. It spread throughout the town as companies of men moved into positions from which they could control not only the movement through the city but access to the Sceir Naid as well. Yet most startling of all was what Julian alone could see. Beyond the meadow where the fairgrounds lay smoldering, up the river road came an army.

Julian flew over the approaching host, noting the colorful banners and pennants though the designs meant nothing to him. He tried to count the men, but he was accustomed to counting only by way of comparison. He could, for instance, tell that this many frogs were more than that many, but he couldn't tell how many men were heading to Durham. He only knew it was many times more than the king had gathered about him in the palace. The Watcher flew back to report what he had seen.

Duke Fitzwarren knew exactly what those troops meant--a chance to salvage his ruined plans. His worthless sons had failed to open the gates, and now it was impossible to know what was going on behind those tall, frowning walls. There should have been enough men loyal to him, not counting his incompetent heirs or Claranides' brigands, to have captured the palace anyway, but something had gone wrong. The men he had sent through the tunnel had reported the church strongly defended and there was no way of knowing if Claranides had carried out his part of the plan. They had never planned to lay siege to the fortress, and with neither siege machines nor engineers it seemed impossible to defeat those imposing battlements. But once the soldiers of Duke Broderick Laighan entered the city, the Sceir Naid would be completely boxed in. He still had the king by the throat.

———————

When Evan related what the Watcher had told him, no one questioned the accuracy of the information. The news brought a renewed immediacy to their actions. If they didn't get control of the palace before those troops arrived it would be impossible to defend the walls against so many, so they hurried on through the corridors and rooms looking for the heart of the treachery that had seized their world.

They found it in the Great Hall. Soldiers guarding the entrance to the audience chamber retreated as the king's party advanced. With a howl of rage, Osric bolted after them, and such was the speed and ferocity of his charge that they were unable to bar the door.

"The king!" someone screamed, and then death was upon them.

The heavy wooden portals thundered back against the walls as the king and his followers stormed into the room. The hall was full of people: Red Guard, palace soldiers and many of the kingdom's nobles were crowded into the alcoves and antechambers surrounding the throne. But the Dukes and Barons were weaponless, their families, wives and children held there by naked steel. And Eochad was there too.

Though outnumbered, the attackers swept into the room like a tide of death, and at the sight of the king, resistance collapsed. Soon Osric and Eochad faced each other beside the royal throne of Glenmara.

Eochad was no coward, but now terror stole his breath. In all the time he had served this king he had never seen such malice in his eyes, never sensed such a fire of wrath and power, and it felt as though that power was draining Eochad's life away. An agonizing cry rose up from his throat to become a maniacal shriek that was abruptly cut short by Osric's sword. The king's seneschal was dead as he hit the floor.

The freed nobles told of being dragged from their rooms by Eochad, their servants slain, possessions looted and families herded into the throne room. Osric explained what he knew to his vassals and then divided his forces into three groups. The first he took to the defense of the walls, Brendan Ceallaigh led the second through the palace to flush out any further resistance and Evan took the third to secure the river gate.

Evan had never been more elated. The strength that coursed through his limbs brought with it a heady, narcotic effect. Not an hour ago he had been at the mercy of Claranides and then the miracle! What would Brian think of him now? What would Aine think?

But here his thoughts strayed into shadow and uncertainty. Lingering doubts brought his concern for Aine's safety to the forefront of his consideration. He snarled as he led his small troop toward the dock where he and Osric had fished as boys. It was Martin's fault that he was taking on so. True to form the boy asked endless questions, most of them concerning Aine Ceallaigh and all of them to the same effect.

"Do we know she is safe?"

He prattled on in this manner until Evan began to feel that Martin cared more for Aine's safety than he did, which in turn made him angry. But it also made him think.

Baron Ceallaigh's words echoed in quiet whispers through his mind, more ominous with each repeating: "In her rooms I should think." *I should think?* Which meant he wasn't certain? Which meant she could be anywhere. His fear grew; his agitation intensified. He ought to turn these men around and find her. But if he did that, and the enemy seized the dock, how would that serve anyone?

On the other hand, if something happened to Aine, what difference did anything else make? Though he tried to be rational about his irrational fears, Martin's insistent questioning highlighted his growing anguish. She hadn't been in the Great Hall, so where else would she be but in her rooms? Perhaps dead, savaged, her sightless eyes staring forever into darkness and the images of the last horrifying moments of her life.

Evan growled to clear his mind of the awful pictures he was painting. The men around him took this as a sign of Evan's rage at the treachery against his brother and their own commitment sharpened--sharpened to the point that when Torgal Umliath came staggering down the hallway chased by a squad of palace guards, they fell upon his pursuers like wild animals.

The guards were torn to pieces in a frenzy of carnage that surprised even those who had accomplished it, adding four more bodies to the already heavy toll of life that marked that morning. Torgal fell into Evan's arms unable to speak, uncomprehending that his former patient was now healthy and strong.

It was some while before he could say anything, but the first words that came from his shaking, gasping voice sent waves of raw terror through Evan.

"Lady Aine..."

"What of Lady Aine?" whispered Evan as the nightmares welled up around him.

In bits and pieces Torgal told the story with all its desperate implications, and Evan's strength was replaced by a fear so great that he found himself paralyzed. Julian said something and flew down the hall toward Torgal's tower. Focusing all his will to control the overpowering despair, Evan followed his Watcher.

———————

They found Aine's bow at the foot of the tower stairs with the bodies of the two men she had felled, mute testimony to her marksmanship. Her discarded quiver became their next clue, and then a cowering, whimpering Guthrum confirmed their worst fears.

Bodies in the livery of the king littered the floor at the end of the corridor. At the dock, two guard boats had been sunk at their moorings, and the king's barge was missing.

There was no sign of Aine.

(Continued in *The Fields of Clon Miarth*)

Glossary

A brief list of pronunciation

NAME	PRONUNCIATION
Aine Ceallaigh	Ayn Kelly
Ascalon	Askálon
Augustus Claes	Augustus Clays
Balinora Mountains	Balinóra Mountains
Bran Mael Morda	Bran Maal Morda
Canorian Pass	Canórian Pass
Claranides	Clara nighdeeze
Dungal	Doongall
Durham	Doórum
Eonacht	Yaánok
Evan MacKeth	Evun Mukéth
Faltigern	Faáltigurn
Glamorth	Glamórth
Glenmara	Glenmaára
Glenne	Glen
Iarlaithe	Eeárleth

Illyria	Illiŕia
Iosa Christus	Yosa Christoos
Ivrian Ceallaigh	Ivrian Kelly
Julian Vorenius	Julian Voréneeus
Kevin Mac Maoilorian	Kevin Mac Mailórian
Klabaga	Klabaága
Moloch	Máalock
O'Byrne	O' Burn
Osric Murchadha	Ozric Mur-kaáda
River Cuinn	River Shawn
River Gabhailin	River Gabáylin
River Aiden	River Áyden
River Orth	River Oarth

Printed in the United States
145661LV00001B/16/A